Tangleton

by

Gordon Ottewell

British Library Cataloguing-in-publication data.
A catalogue record for this book is available from
the British Library.
ISBN 0 9526031 8 7

First published in 2005 by Green Branch Press, Kencot
Lodge, Kencot, Lechlade, Gloucestershire GL7 3QX,
United Kingdom.
Tel. 01367 860588. Fax 01367 860619.

Typeset by Green Branch Press.

Printed and bound by Stoate and Bishop Printers,
Cheltenham.

Cover picture: Geoff Thomas

TANGLETON

by
Gordon Ottewell

CONTENTS

Chapters

1. The Strange Boy.

2. Discoveries.

3. Puzzles and Problems.

4. Night Adventure.

5. Accident!

6. The Rescue.

7. The Colonel.

8. Schemes and Surprises.

9. Perkins.

10. The Visitor.

11. The Wanderer Returns.

12. The Dream.

13. Fire!

14. Celebration.

For my dear grandchildren, Jack, Megan and Harry.

A Cotswold Village.

Chapter 1

The Strange Boy

Max stood by the open window of his new bedroom. It was almost dark outside. The shadowy forms of tall spreading trees crowded in on either side, the leafy outer branches swaying slightly in the evening breeze. Gradually, as he looked out, the shiny rim of the full moon rose into view out of the gloom, bathing the garden in silvery light as it climbed higher into the sky. Yes, he was glad after all that they had left the city and come to Tangleton. He had spent holidays in the country but this was different. Now he had come to live here. It was the beginning of a new life, a real adventure.

The silence was almost uncanny. Not a sound disturbed the air, just as though the fields and woods were sleeping. Tomorrow he would explore the garden and the old buildings. He could just make out their dim outline beyond the apple trees below his window. Dad had always wanted a house with outbuildings, suitable to convert into a workshop, where he could indulge in his passion for tinkering with anything mechanical that he could lay his hands on.

As he turned from the window, something caught his attention. The window of the middle building, a low structure smaller than the other two, was slowly opening! He stood rooted to the spot in fascination as a hand grasped the sill. Within seconds, a bespectacled face appeared and a boy, no bigger than himself, leapt nimbly from the window, quickly closing it after him, and disappeared in the moonlight under the trees. Surprise gave way to indignation in Max's mind. Of all the cheek! Whoever he was, the boy had no right to treat their property as though it were his own. Anyone could see that the house was inhabited. He was about to go to Jenny's room to ask if she had seen the incident when he realised that his sister's window faced the front of the house. He'd tell Dad tomorrow instead. He wouldn't be very pleased to know that the local children used his buildings as a playground.

Next morning, Max woke with a start. A shaft of sunlight pierced his room through a chink in the curtain and dazzled his eyes. He groped for his bedside clock. Ten past nine! He knew he'd been tired after yesterday's activity but this was ridiculous. Scrambling out of bed, he padded across to Jenny's room. Sure enough, it was empty. She might have called him! He washed and dressed quickly and went downstairs, to find his mother and sister finishing breakfast.

"Hello, Mum – where's Dad?"

"Gone over to Chipping Burton to get some curtain fittings," came the reply. "Did you sleep well?"

"Too well." Max said, rubbing his eyes. "I intended getting up early. Wanted to explore the garden and the buildings." Suddenly he recalled the boy with glasses. Should he tell them? No – best wait until Dad got back.

"Well, you've got all day to do that," his mother smiled. "You go with him, Jenny. Fresh country air will do you both good."

They found that the nearest outbuilding to the house, which their father intended using as a garage, was open, but the other two were locked and a search failed to locate the keys.

"I expect Dad's got them," Jenny said. "We can look inside when he gets back. Let's leave the garden until later and walk up the lane. I want to find out where it leads to." Max was examining the window from which the boy had jumped. The catch was broken and it opened easily. He peered inside but could make out nothing except for a few wooden crates and a stone-slabbed floor strewn with rubbish.

"Come on," Jenny urged.

The lane twisted tortuously uphill, hemmed in on either side by tall hedges, scarcely wide enough for any vehicle bigger than a car and with only a few passing places at intervals. It was the last week in August, and the hedgebanks were covered with flowers, many of which were completely unfamiliar to the children. There was a constant hum of insects in the air, and from time to time large, beautifully coloured butterflies drifted along ahead of them, as though beckoning them to follow. Soon, they were plagued by swarms of flies, which seemed to have been lying in wait for them and defied all their attempts to drive them away. Max began to tire and flopped down on the grassy bank.

"I vote we go back – we don't seem to be getting anywhere," he gasped, flailing his arms in exasperation at his tormentors.

"You can go back if you want to," Jenny said disdainfully, tossing her head, "but I'm going on. It must level out sometime – can't go on climbing for ever. Anyway, I bet there's a super view from the top."

Reluctantly, Max rose to his feet. "Suppose I'll have to come too," he said grudgingly. "You know what Mum always says about not wandering off alone."

"Please yourself!" his sister flung over her shoulder. After a few minutes more of steady climbing, they found to their relief that the road did level out as Jenny had predicted and as they rounded a bend, a tiny cottage came into view by the roadside. It was built of the same yellow-coloured stone as their own house but also had a roof of stone tiles, the weight of which had caused the roof timbers to sag alarmingly in the middle. Tall trees enclosed the tiny front garden, in which grew a tangled mass of shrubs and flowering plants. They could see an untidy collection of rickety sheds behind the cottage. As they drew near, the sound of hammering could be heard coming from one of the sheds.

"I'm thirsty," Max whispered. "Shall we ask for a drink?"

Jenny looked doubtful. "I don't think we should. Let's hurry – come on." They were almost level with the cottage gate when a strange voice brought them to an abrupt halt.

"You the kids what's come to live in the witch's 'ouse?" Max wheeled round. Watching them over the fence was the boy with glasses.

~~~~~~~~

Jenny too, spun round in surprise. "I don't know what you mean," she replied coldly, quickly recovering her poise. "What business is it of yours, anyway?"

The boy blinked at her through his glasses, reminding Max of an owl he had once seen at a wildlife park. He didn't seem in the least put out by Jenny's manner, however, and turned to Max. " 'ow old are you?"

Max could not evade such a direct question. "Ten," he replied mechanically. "I was ten last month."

The boy blinked again. "An' 'ow old's she?" He nodded in Jenny's direction.

"If you *must* know, I shall be twelve on the twenty-eighth of September," Jenny announced curtly before turning to her brother. "Come on, Max, let's go."

Max, however, was still puzzling over the boy's opening remark. "We've just moved into the house down the lane, if that's what you mean," he said, studying the boy's face intently.

"Yes, and it's called Oaklands," Jenny added in her most crushing manner.

"Me an' Kit allus calls it the witch's 'ouse," the boy said. "Scared to pass it, we were."

"Kit?" Max repeated.

"Me sister," the boy explained. "She's only seven. I'm ten – like you."

Jenny gave a snort of contempt. "Sounds a silly name for a house. Why call it that, anyway?"

The boy blinked again, recoiling his neck in an even more bird-like manner. " 'Cos a witch lived there," he said solemnly.

Jenny gave a mocking laugh. "A witch! And I expect she had a cauldron and a broomstick and a big black cat and . . ."

"Yeh, she did," the boy interrupted. "Well, she 'ad this whoppin' big cat – an' black it were too. She called 'im Perkins. Still around 'ere somewhere, our dad says. Gone wild by now, I 'spect."

"But it doesn't make someone a witch, just because she

11

has a black cat," Max insisted.

"No – but Miss Ferriday were!" The boy's voice dropped to an urgent whisper. Max found himself being drawn towards the fence. Even Jenny stood alert, listening. The boy's eyes looked even larger and rounder behind his thick glasses. "She lived on 'er own in that great big 'ouse – 'er an' 'er cat. Lived there years. Dressed in funny, ole-fashioned clothes, she did. Never went out. Sort of. . ." "Hermit?" Max suggested.

"Recluse," said Jenny.

The boy blinked. "Yeh. Well, anyway, she could cast spells an' one day. . . ?"

"Uh!" Jenny snorted in disbelief. "Whoever heard of witches casting spells on people these days – ridiculous!"

" 'taint dikkerluss!" the boy insisted. "She cast a spell on the Colonel – an' it worked! Ask anybody in Tangleton – they'll tell yer."

"The Colonel – who's he?" Max demanded, struggling to follow the boy's story.

"Colonel Ferriday, Miss Ferriday's brother," the boy said. " 'e owns all this land – for miles an' miles around. The village an' all. Our dad says that Miss Ferriday an' the Colonel 'ad a row an' she cast a spell on 'im. Said 'e'd never smile again – an' 'e 'asn't!" He looked from Max to Jenny solemnly, more owl-like than ever, Max thought.

"Well, I don't believe a word of it," Jenny said contemptuously, turning away. "Come on, Max, it's time we were going."

"Just a moment," Max said accusingly. "How come if you were so scared of Miss Ferriday's – our – house, you came poking around last night?"

Jenny looked in surprise from her brother to the boy.

12

" 'ow – 'ow did you know?" he stammered.

"Because I saw you – watched you come through our shed window." Max replied.

The boy squirmed uncomfortably. "Well – I'm not scared now," he mumbled, "– not now she's gone."

"But what were you doing on our property, anyway?" Max persisted, determined to know the whole truth.

The boy hung his head guiltily. "I – I – was lookin' for – bottles."

"Bottles?" repeated Jenny, who had been listening to the boys' conversation in growing bewilderment.

"What kind of bottles?" asked Max, also puzzled.

The boy's face suddenly brightened. "Ol' bottles, made out of funny green glass, an' them with marbles in – an', well – you know."

"We certainly don't know," Jenny contradicted. "We've ab-solutely no idea what you're talking about."

Suddenly the boy darted to the gate and threw it open. "Come an' see my c'lection. It's in the shed. Won't take long."

Jenny looked doubtfully at her brother. They hesitated, un-sure what to do.

"Ple-ease," the boy pleaded.

"All right," Jenny said reluctantly. "But we can only stay a few minutes."

The boy led the way along a winding path by the side of the cottage to a dilapidated wooden shed, one of several scat-tered over an expanse of derelict land. Jenny stared at the words JOES. PLEEZE NOK, in lurid red paint on the door.

"My moo-zeem!" the boy explained proudly, stepping inside.

"You're Joe?" Max asked.

The boy nodded.

"My name's Max Davis – and my sister's called Jenny," Max informed him.

"My sister's Kit," the boy said, "– an' my little brother's called George. 'e's only four."

The shed had no windows and it took the children's eyes some time to adjust to the gloomy interior. Joe's collection was displayed on a number of rough wooden boards, balanced precariously on rickety packing crates. It consisted of pieces of rock, some containing fossils; birds' feathers and nests; as assortment of bones, including skulls of various kinds; fragments of pottery, clay pipes – and bottles. There were bottles everywhere. Some were hanging on strings from nails in the roof, others were arranged in groups on the floor, yet others were filled with water and holding dejected-looking bunches of wild flowers.

Max, who had recently become interested in bird watching, was immediately attracted by the feathers. Some, long and quill-like, were mounted on scraps of cardboard, while soft, downy feathers were pressed between a strip of coloured wallpaper and a sheet of glass. He badly wanted to examine them closer but hesitated on noticing the words DOANT TUTCH, scrawled in chalk on a piece of wood nearby.

"Oh, take no notice o' that," the boy assured him. "That's put there for Kit an' George." He laughed. "George can't read, o' course, but 'e knows what it means!"

Jenny stared at the bottles. They were of every conceivable size and shape, chiefly of a greenish-coloured glass which reminded her of the sea. No two bottles were alike; each one had some distinctive feature – a tear-like mark, a series of unusual lines along the neck, or a rainbow pattern incorporated into the glass. There were tall, elegant wine bottles, squat and bulbous jars, ornately-fashioned bottles with lettering along their sides, and tiny octagonal bottles with roughly-finished rims. There were dark green bottles too, and rotund jars made from luminous yellow-brown glass. A narrow shelf opposite the door was lined with stone jars, richly-coloured in brown, yellow and dark blue, with decorative lettering and intricate designs.

"Them's ginger beers," Joe said proudly, as Jenny's eyes lingered along the shelf. "Keep 'em up there outa George's reach – jus' in case!"

"But where did you get them?" Jenny asked.

Joe gave an owl-like blink in the half-light. "Dug 'em up, mostly. Found one or two in ol' buildins though." He turned to rummage behind the door and offered Jenny a somewhat unexceptional-looking white jar. "Found this las' night in your shed," he said guiltily. "Wouldn't 'ave taken it if I'd known you'd come ta live there. Thought per'aps the ole wi' – Miss Ferriday – might 'ave kept some ole bottles in 'er sheds. Would 'ave been a pity if they'd 'ave been chucked away."

Jenny regarded the jar uncertainly. "You'd better keep it", she said. "After all, you found it. I don't suppose I'd have noticed it anyway."

"It ain't a very good 'un really," Joe conceded. "Tell ya what – you pick one o' my c'lection. Any bottle ya like. Go on." Jenny was quite taken aback. The boy obviously wanted to please but she felt she couldn't take one of his best bottles.

She compromised by choosing one of the dainty little green ink bottles. "I'll have this one, then, if you're really sure. Thanks very much."

Max, whose gaze had been feasting on the feathers, was also persuaded to choose a specimen to keep. They bade farewell to the boy, who waved to them from the fence as they set off back down the lane.

"Come again," he called after them. "We'll go explorin'. There's lots ta see."

They walked for some time in silence. "What a strange boy," Jenny said at last. "I've never met anyone so – unusual."

"I like him." Max replied emphatically.

Jenny looked again at the quaint little green bottle nestling in her hand. "Yes. Yes – I suppose I do too."

Chapter 2

Discoveries

Mr Davis suggested clearing out the garage after lunch and the children readily agreed to help. Although a spacious building, big enough to hold two cars, it had clearly not been used for that purpose. It was piled high with useless clutter, a good deal of which they were able to burn on a fire in the garden. Jenny kept a sharp lookout for old bottles but all she found were a few ancient preserving jars, made from clear glass, with rusty metal tops, which were consigned to the bin.

"What kind of person was Miss Ferriday, Dad?" Max asked.

His father looked up enquiringly. "I've really no idea. Never met her. Why do you ask?"

"Oh, just wondered." He was half-inclined to tell his father about their meeting with Joe, leaving out the episode of his secret search for bottles, but decided against it, for the present at least.

Jenny was obviously thinking along similar lines. "Just imagine living in a big old house like this, all on her own." she said reflectively.

Their father put down his dustpan and brush. "Yes, she was a queer old soul from what I've heard," he said. "No servants, no companion, no car, no telephone, even. And the way she neglected this place! It'll take me months to put it to rights – and leave me in the red at the bank too!"

"Workers' official tea break!" their mother called from the kitchen doorway.

Mr Davis needed no second bidding. "Come on, you two, you've earned a break. We'll finish off later," Max dusted himself down and followed his father indoors.

"I'll not be a minute", Jenny called. She had just started rummaging through a battered old tea chest, apparently full of end-rolls of bilious-coloured wallpaper and tatty wallpaper pattern books, and was determined to finish the task. Suddenly she paused. Tucked away between two of the books was a smaller book with a blotched and faded yellow cover. She picked it up and with an effort managed to read the title, hand-written in a distinctive tyle: *The Natural History of Tangleton Park, by Rachel Ferriday. 1923.*

Slowly, and with suppressed excitement, she opened the book. The title page, also in beautiful script, bore a watercolour painting of an elegant country house, standing in open parkland, with an ornamental lake in the foreground. Tall, stately trees stretching away into the distance completed the picture. Jenny gazed at it with wonder. Art was not only her favourite subject at school but also her hobby too. She immediately recognised the skill of the artist whose work lay before her. If only she could paint like that! Trembling with anticipation, she turned over the pages. Each bore a picture of a plant or animal identified in the park, together with the artist's observations. Trees, flowers, grasses, butterflies, birds, mammals – fishes even! And each creature depicted in lifelike detail, the natural colouring perfectly reproduced. What skill – and what time it must have taken! And to think that it might well have been thrown with the rubbish on to the fire! As though in a dream, she turned and made her way indoors, clutching her discovery.

What had been intended as a brief refreshment break ended up as a leisurely examination of Jenny's amazing find. The children's parents were just as thrilled as Jenny and Max, everyone agreeing that the book was a superb work of art.

"Just look at these birds!" Max exclaimed, gingerly turning the pages. "Nuthatch and great-spotted woodpecker! And great crested grebe, too! It says they bred on the lake."

"Probably do still," said his father, studying the picture. "I'm no expert on birds but from what I've been told, the old Colonel's let the estate go to rack and ruin. Become something of a recluse, apparently, like his sister."

The children exchanged glances and Max nodded, indicating that Jenny should tell their parents about Joe.

"We met a boy this morning," Jenny began. "He lives in a cottage up the lane. He told us that . . ." she paused and took a deep breath before continuing, " . . . that the local people think that Miss Ferriday was a witch, and that she cast a spell on her brother, the Colonel, so that he can never smile again." They looked from one parent to the other expectantly.

At last, their father's face creased into a playful grin. "I've heard some odd tales about these parts, but that one really does take the biscuit!" he chuckled. "Casting spells – the old boy doomed never to smile again. Takes some beating, that does!"

Mrs Davis puckered her brow thoughtfully. "Yes, but it's easy to see how such superstitions come about," she said quietly. "After all, when a brother and sister quarrel . . . which they must have done, years ago . . . and both end up living lonely, miserable lives, people are bound to speculate on why it happened. That's how gossip and rumour grew into folk lore, I suppose."

Mr Davis nudged Max's elbow. "You'd better not risk quarrelling with your sister," he advised in a loud whisper. "She'll be sure to cast a spell on you!" He twisted his face into a witch-like grimace, prompting Jenny to kick his ankle under the table.

Mrs Davis, who had been slowly turning the pages of the book, held up a picture of a dragonfly resting on a water lily leaf. "These paintings are exquisite!" she said. "We must find out whether Miss Ferriday would like the book back. It must have got amongst that clutter by mistake. I suppose it belongs to her legally anyway."

"I wouldn't know," Mr Davis said, "but you're quite right, dear. I'm popping over to Chipping Burton tomorrow to see our solicitor. I'll have a word with him about it. He'll know how to contact Miss Ferriday."

"Did Miss Ferriday buy another house?" Max asked.

"No, she moved into an old peoples' apartment somewhere Chipping Burton way when she couldn't cope here any longer," Mr Davis replied. "I bet she'll be glad to have her book though. It must have lain there for years, judging by the state of its cover. It seem's a pity it wasn't published – it's certainly good enough."

"Yes indeed," Mrs Davis agreed, "You'd better make the most of it while we still have it, you two. If you intend being an artist, Jenny, and you a naturalist, Max, you couldn't have a better model."

Jenny gazed absently at the open page before her. "It seems such a pity. To think that the old lady had all this talent and allowed it to go to waste."

"She could have become famous, you mean?" Max asked.

His sister frowned. "No – well, not just that. It's a shame that she shut herself away, instead of giving other people – and herself – pleasure from her skill."

Their father rose from the table, ready to resume their task. "Of course, she may have painted scores of pictures," he said with a smile. "They're probably hidden around the place some-where – who knows?"

"Highly unlikely, I should think," Mrs Davis said. "I sense somehow that this lovely book contains the entire work of a very talented lady."

"I'm going to keep a sharp lookout anyway," Max said, "– just in case."

They searched carefully through all that remained to be cleared from the first out-building but found nothing of value. The two other buildings yielded only a few empty packing crates, broken furniture and a miscellaneous collection of flower pots and broken garden tools. Max could not hide his disappointment.

"Anything worth having was sold at the auction, remember," Mr Davis said. "It was purely luck that the book was missed."

It proved to be a wet evening and the children settled down to examine Miss Ferriday's book in detail. Eventually they discovered that what at first sight appeared to be a folded page midway through the volume was in fact a picture map of the entire locality, showing the market town of Chipping Burton, the village of Tangleton, and the Hall, standing in its extensive park. Miss Ferriday had painstakingly included a vast amount of detail, both with brush and pen and the children were soon able to find their bearings.

Max craned forward intently. "There's our house – look – Oaklands!" he pointed. "– and here's the lane leading up towards . . ."

"Keeper's Cottage!" Jenny interrupted.

"That'll be the cottage where Joe lives," Max mused. "His father must be a gamekeeper. That explains how he's managed to collect all those feathers and bones and so on."

Jenny looked doubtful. "But Dad said that the Colonel had let the estate fall into neglect. If that's the case, I shouldn't think there would be a gamekeeper now."

Max nodded. "This map's over sixty years old anyway. There are bound to have been lots of changes since then."

Jenny continued to trace the line of the lane with her finger. "See – if we had kept going beyond Joe's cottage, we'd have come to Park Cottages – a row of four. I wonder if anyone of our age lives in one of them."

"Quite likely, I should think," said Max. "I'll ask Joe – he's sure to know."

Jenny's finger stopped. "Here's the lodge at the entrance to the hall drive. . ."

" . . . and there's the hall," Max exclaimed, leapfrogging his sister's finger with his own and pointing to a miniature representation of the building depicted on the title page of the book. Although the map did not appear to be drawn strictly to scale, they could see that the park covered a vast area of ground.

"It must be teeming with wild life!" Max said longingly.

"'And what a wonderful place for sketching and painting," added Jenny, " – not that I could ever hope to reach Miss Ferriday's standard."

Max began tracing the route back towards Oaklands. "Joe would love to see this book," he said as his finger passed Keeper's Cottage. "I'll go up and see him tomorrow morning – get him to come down."

"The sooner the better," Jenny agreed. "Miss Ferriday will want it back pretty quickly when she hears about it, I expect."

~~~~~~~~

Max set off for Keeper's Cottage soon after breakfast. It was a warm, clear morning and the leaves, still wet from the heavy overnight rain, glistened and sparkled in the sunshine. He recalled with surprise how tired he had felt on the previous morning; it had seemed a long walk then. Now, however, the cottage soon came into view. He craned his neck to see over the fence, half-expecting Joe to appear but there was no sign. Hesitantly opening the gate, Max followed the winding path leading behind the cottage. Seeing the kitchen door open, he knocked and waited. The tiny kitchen was plainly furnished but neatly kept. He noticed a shotgun suspended from hooks in the ceiling; a clock ticked quietly somewhere within. His knock, however, remained unanswered. Perhaps Joe had gone up to Park Cottages to see a friend. Disappointed, he turned back towards the gate. Suddenly a thought struck him. Maybe Joe was in his museum. He approached the shed and lifted the latch.

"An' just what d'ya think you're doin?" He spun round to

see a dark, bearded man, wearing a cap, a rough green pullover and wellingtons, standing blocking his path. The limp form of a rabbit dangled from his hand.

"I – I – was just trying to find – " Max began.

The man cut him short. "You've no business snoopin' round 'ere. Be off with ya – an' quick!"

Max felt the colour rush to his cheeks. "But I wasn't snooping!" he insisted. "Honestly I wasn't. I was just looking –."

"You 'eard what I said!" the man's voice rose threateningly. "I've put up wi' a lot, but I'm not 'avin' folks – or their kids – pokin' their noses inta my affairs. Nah – clear off!"

Max could see that it was useless to argue. The man was clearly not prepared to listen. Heart pounding, he made his way back to the gate.

"An' ya can tell them as sent ya!" the man shouted, waving his fist in the air. "They can do what they like 'ere when I've gone but till then it's private property – an' don't you dare forget it!"

Upset and bewildered, Max half-walked, half ran back down the lane. What on earth had the man meant? Surely he could see that he intended no harm? And where was Joe? And the rest of the family? It didn't make sense. Deep in troubled thought, he slowed down and finally came to a stop. Why was he running away? Perhaps his friend was up at Park Cottages after all. There was no harm in finding out, anyway. No one, not even the angry man, could prevent him from walking past the cottage. He turned back determinedly. Even so, he felt his muscles tense as the cottage came once more into view. Suppose the man was mentally ill – violent, even? He willed himself to dismiss such alarming fears. Approaching the cottage

24

gate, he found himself treading on tiptoe almost, ready to turn and run at the first sign of anything threatening. But to his relief, there was neither sight nor sound of the man. Thankfully he left the cottage behind and stepped out with renewed purpose. From what he could recall of Miss Ferriday's map, Park Cottages were only a short distance beyond Keeper's Cottage. And if Joe wasn't there, he would ask someone at the cottages about the strange man. He was determined to solve the mystery of Keeper's Cottage once and for all. If only Jenny had been there! He had to admit that his sister had a flair for reasoning things out, somehow – and she knew a fair bit about handling grown-ups, too. Still, it was no use wishing. She had stayed behind, keeping her promise to help Mum with leftover unpacking of some kind. He was alone and he had to make his own decisions unaided for once. Whatever happened he'd have plenty to tell them all when he got back home.

He had expected to see Park Cottages coming into view by now. According to the map, they stood on the right hand side of the lane, just before the lodge at the entrance to the drive leading to the hall. Perhaps the map had not been drawn accurately after all. Miss Ferriday may have been a brilliant artist and an observant naturalist, but . . . He pulled up abruptly. Before him stood the lodge, looking exactly as it had on the map, except that its windows were shattered and several tiles were missing from its roof. But where were Park Cottages? Max stood dumbfounded.

"This is crazy! A row of four cottages can't just disappear. There must be some explanation," he said out loud. Perhaps his memory was playing tricks. Maybe they were beyond the lodge. He continued past the deserted building and the unkempt entrance to the drive but soon the lane became a mere cart track before finally petering out at a field gate.

Utterly baffled by now, he began retracing his steps before pulling up abruptly by the abandoned lodge. Of course! Why hadn't he thought of it before! Slowly he made his way back towards Keeper's Cottage, peering as he went into the tangle of vegetation along the side of the lane. Suddenly, something caught his eye. Bent almost double, he pushed his way through the dense undergrowth and at last reached the vertical stone he had glimpsed from the lane. A gatepost! He scrambled on, wincing as straggling briars tore at his clothes and sinewy roots did their utmost to trip him headlong. Again he stopped. He had reached the junction of two low crumbling walls, across which lay a huge rotting wooden beam.   Beneath the tangle of nettles and pungent-smelling weeds, he could see stones, broken tiles and fragments of glass strewn everywhere.

"Park Cottages – or what's left of them," he said aloud, with grim satisfaction as he stumbled back towards the lane.

Chapter 3

Puzzles and Problems

An air of gloom had settled over the Davis family. They had eaten lunch but remained seated despondently round the table, each member absorbed in his or her own particular private thoughts. Max had just finished relating his morning's experiences. Any sense of achievement he had felt over solving the mystery of Park Cottages was overshadowed by his disappointment at not finding Joe.

Mr Davis broke the silence. "The man you saw, Max, was obviously Joe's father," he said, a troubled frown creasing his brow. "Though why he should behave so unpleasantly, I just can't understand."

"But where was Joe?" Max insisted. " – and his mother and brother and sister? The place seemed deserted, just as though. . . "

Jenny interrupted him. "Of course, we've no proof that he *has* a mother, have we?" she pointed out. "I don't recall Joe mentioning her."

"No – no he didn't, that's true," Max agreed.

"They could have been anywhere, come to that", Mr Davis pointed out. " – gone to town shopping, perhaps, or out visiting friends. It doesn't necessarily follow that because they weren't around when you called, they're in some sort of trouble."

Max still felt uneasy, however, "I just sensed that something was wrong, that's all."

His father gave him a reassuring pat on the shoulder. "Well, I'm driving into Chipping Burton this afternoon to see our solicitor and to meet Jenny's new headmaster. I'll make a few discreet enquiries. Someone's sure to know your friend's family. What did you say they're called?"

Max hesitated. "I don't know. I didn't ask."

"We only know him as Joe," Jenny explained. "and he has a sister called Kit ."

"Yes, and a younger brother called George," Max added.

"I don't suppose I shall need to know their name to find out something about them," Mr Davis said. "Everybody seems to know everybody else's business in an area like this. Seeing that they live at Keeper's Cottage, and from how you describe the man's appearance, Max, he's obviously the Colonel's gamekeeper."

"That poor rabbit – ugh!" said Jenny with a shudder, recalling her brother's description of the angry man.

"Yes, I'm afraid that some of the ways of country people may seem cruel to you," her father said. "It's bound to take you some time to understand them, and even then you won't necessarily agree with everything they do. But I hope that in time you'll find that there's a great deal to be said in favour of country life."

Jenny caught her mother's eye. "Tell them about this morning, Mum," she urged. Max and his father turned towards Mrs

Davis, who had sat in an unusually subdued manner throughout the discussion.

"Jenny and I walked down to the village this morning," she began. "We couldn't help noticing how neglected and forlorn the place appeared. The houses must have looked lovely years ago, but now half of them are crumbling to pieces."

"Empty, many of them – have been for years, I'd say," Jenny added. "Weeds sprouting out of the thatch and the stonework. The whole place seems to be dying."

"And it's not only that," Mrs Davis continued. "It's affecting the people too. We went into the little village store to buy a few things. The lady behind the counter seemed pleasant enough at first but when I asked her the times of the church services, she mumbled something about them being discontinued since last year and made it clear that she didn't want to carry on the conversation."

"Now tell them about meeting the other lady, Mum," Jenny prompted.

"On our way back," Mrs Davis continued, "we met a lady with a boy about your age, Max. I spoke to her and she replied in the normal way. She asked if we were on holiday here but when I told her that we had come to live here and that my son would be starting at the village school next week, she blurted out something about the school being closed down next year and turned away."

Mr Davis looked puzzled. "But the headmistress made no mention of that when she replied to our letter asking for Max to be enrolled," he said.

Mrs Davis bit her lip. "There may be nothing in it, of course, but it's yet another reason for feeling . . ."

" . . . that this is a miserable village!" Jenny cut in bitterly.

Mrs Davis decided to travel over to Chipping Burton with her husband during the afternoon but the children chose to remain at home. Jenny had collected a few specimens of wild flowers on the way back from the village and was eager to try her hand at painting them. Max, meanwhile, set about unpacking his bird books, after which he settled down to draw some of the birds he had already identified around Oaklands. They worked in absorbed silence for some time before Jenny suddenly looked up.

"I read a story once about a country where the people were all terribly unhappy because the king had died and his two sons had quarrelled and split the kingdom in half between them."

Max, who was patiently trying to capture the correct shape of a bullfinch's beak, grimaced. "So what?" he said absently. "What's that got to do with – with – anything?"

"Don't you see?" Jenny went on. "This village is like that. Can't you remember what Joe said about the Colonel quarrelling with Miss Ferriday?"

Max attempted to imitate his father's impression of a sinister old crone: "I hereby cast a spell on my horrible brother so that he shall never smile again . . ."

"That's not even remotely funny!" Jenny snapped in annoyance. "Try being serious for once. This is important."

"But I don't see how the story you read fits Tangleton," Max insisted.

Jenny went on impatiently: "Listen. It fits because the two most important people here – the Colonel and his sister – have quarrelled and they're both too stubborn to make it up."

"So?" Max asked, trying hard to follow his sister's reasoning.

"So – they're both unhappy and their behaviour is making everyone else unhappy too," Jenny went on. "– and I don't see how the quarrel can be patched up unless Miss Ferriday comes back."

Max was bewildered. "But she can't come back to Oaklands now,' he insisted"

"I know that, stupid!" Jenny snapped, picking up her brush once more. "I only wish I could think of a way of solving the problem."

"But it's not our affair, is it?" Max went on. "We can't interfere – they'd soon tell us to mind our own business. I've been told that already today, remember." He recalled his encounter with the gamekeeper with a shudder. Jenny continued painting. "Even so, someone should do something," she said, "otherwise things will go from bad to worse. All the people will leave and the village will just crumble away."

Max pictured the remains of Park Cottages, decaying under the bushes. "If Joe's cottage is abandoned, Oaklands will be the only house left between the village and the hall."

"What makes you say that?" Jenny demanded, swinging round, brush in hand.

"Say what?" Max asked, puzzled by her sudden change of mood.

"About Joe's cottage being abandoned,"

"I – I – don't know," Max confessed. "Except that soon there won't be any people left near the hall and then –"

"That's it!" Jenny exclaimed. "You've got it!"

Max was at a loss to understand what she meant. "Have I? What have I got?"

"The reason why Joe wasn't at home this morning – and the reason why his father was so horrid," Jenny declared.

Max, however, was still far from clear what exactly it was that he had stumbled upon.

"Look, it stands to sense!" Jenny said, throwing down her brush and jumping up. "You said that the man – Joe's father – complained about people snooping on his property and went on to say that they could do what they want when he'd gone. Don't you see? The Colonel must have told him to leave, so that his cottage will fall down like the rest!"

"But why should the Colonel want everyone to leave?" Max persisted.

Jenny looked away, her sparkle gone. "Probably because he's ill, or because he's like his sister – prefers living like a recluse."

Max looked horrified. "But what if Joe's family can't find anywhere else to live? What'll happen then, do you think?"

"I don't know," Jenny confessed, her voice troubled. "I just don't know."

~~~~~~~~~

Their parents returned home soon afterwards. The children rushed outside as soon as they heard the crunch of car tyres on the gravel drive.

"Got some news for you both," their father said as they helped to carry the shopping indoors.

"Yes, we've had quite a busy afternoon, one way and another," their mother said, sinking down into an easy chair and kicking off her shoes.

"Joe – what about Joe?" Max clamoured. "Were you able

to find out . . . ”

Mr Davis rested a firm, reassuring hand on his son's shoulder. "Now, calm down, old fellow," he said quietly. "Take it easy and I'll tell you everything I know." The children sat down and waited expectantly. "Your friend Joe is the gamekeeper's son, as I suspected," Mr Davis began. "The keeper's name is Pegler, and he's lived at Keeper's Cottage for several years. Mrs Pegler died soon after the youngest child was born." Jenny's lip quivered. "Apart from a butler and an elderly cook/housekeeper, both of whom live in at the hall, Pegler is the last of the Colonel's staff," Mr Davis continued.

"And he won't be there long," Jenny said in a dull whisper.

Mrs Davis looked at her keenly. "How do you know that, Jenny?"

"I just do, that's all," Jenny replied, her eyes downcast.

"As a matter of fact, you're right," Mr Davis said grimly. "It seems that Colonel Ferriday is determined to drive away everybody for miles around, though exactly why is difficult to say."

Jenny was near to tears by now. "It's because he's a cruel, stubborn old man – that's why!"

"Everything points to that, Jenny, I agree," Mr Davis said, "but until we know all the facts we shouldn't . . ."

"Facts!" Jenny burst out. "What facts are there to know? Joe's family have no mother and soon they'll have no home either. It's wicked – wicked!" She ran from the room, stifling a sob. Mrs Davis followed her upstairs. Father and son sat in brooding silence. All the excitement and anticipation of their move to the country seemed to have disappeared. Eventually, they heard movement in the room above and Jenny and her mother returned. Max noticed that his sister was still dabbing her eyes with her handkerchief.

Mr Davis waited until his wife and daughter were again settled. "You are quite right to be concerned about Joe and his family, Jenny," he said. "Mum and I are too, and so of course is Max. He paused. "Our problem is – how can we help? After all, we've never even met Mr Pegler, or any of his children."

"You'd like Joe, Dad, I know you would," Max said earnestly. "He's rather – well, strange, in a way but . . ."

"He cares about – things," Jenny said bitterly.

Their mother looked from one to the other with an understanding smile. "We know that if you like him, we would too," she said.

"We've news about Miss Ferriday, if you're interested," Mr Davis said. "We've managed to get her new address." He produced a card. "I learned something else rather surprising too. The Colonel tried to buy this house. He offered more than we did to get it but his sister refused to sell it to him."

"Probably did it to spite him," Max said. "Talk about children quarrelling – those two behave ten times worse than children!"

Mrs Davis wrinkled her nose, a habit she had when deep in thought. "Perhaps. Or could it be that she didn't want Oaklands to suffer the same fate as all the rest?"

"Maybe – but only because it was hers!" Max said hotly.

"I think you may be judging Miss Ferriday rather harshly, Max," his mother replied. "You see, on the way back from town we called at the school house in the village to see the headmistress. In view of what we had been told by the lady

34

Jenny and I met earlier, we wanted to make sure that the school would be remaining open . . . "

"And will it?" Max demanded.

"Yes – for the time being," Mrs Davis replied, "but Miss Keynes said that if the houses continue to fall into decay, its future is very doubtful, in fact . . . "

Jenny was growing increasingly impatient with the direction the conversation was taking. "But what has all this to do with Miss Ferriday?" she interrupted.

"I'm coming to that, Jenny," her mother said. "Miss Keynes said that Miss Ferriday was a very good friend of the school until recent years. She used to invite the children up to Oaklands for nature walks and picnics. They thought the world of her."

Their father took up the story. "Miss Keynes thinks that Miss Ferriday sold us the house because of you."

"Us?" the children exclaimed, almost in unison.

"In other words, because of her love of children," Mrs Davis said. "Miss Keynes knew the old lady well in the days before she cut herself off from the world and she thinks that she wanted to know that young people were living at Oaklands."

Mr Davis held up the card. "We can write to her now that we have her address," he said. "I expect that she'll want her book back. It should revive some happy memories."

"*I'll* write to her," Jenny announced, her voice back to its customary decisiveness. "After all, *I* found her book, didn't I?" She looked from one parent to the other and then at her brother. "It's only right, isn't it?"

Chapter 4

Night Adventure

Max found sleep impossible. He lay in the darkness, his mind tormented by worry. What could he do to help Joe and his family? It was unthinkable that the Peglers should be turned out of their home and have nowhere else to go. His father had pointed out that Mr Pegler should have little difficulty in getting another post – good gamekeepers were always in demand – but Max found that little consolation. It wasn't fair that a man and his three young children should be faced with such worry. And all because of the stupid obstinacy of one wealthy old man.

He knew that his parents were deeply concerned about the matter and that they would probably think of some way in which they could help. Jenny, too, was sure to come up with some ideas. She had gone up to her room early to write her letter to Miss Ferriday. Max understood his sister's determined character. He knew that she would include in her letter a strong plea to the old lady to do something about the cloud of unhappiness hanging over Tangleton. But what about Joe, and his young sister and brother? He *had* to think of some way to help – but how?

He must have fallen into a troubled sleep at last, for he

awoke abruptly and sat up in bed. What was that? Had he been dreaming, or had an unfamiliar sound roused him from his sleep? He sat bolt upright in the darkness, listening. Yes, there it was again, a sharp rattling sound against his window! Wide awake by now, he slipped out of bed and tiptoeing to the window, pulled the curtain aside and looked out. It was still dark. He could just make out the shadowy forms of the apple trees below his window. Just then, another rattling volley sounded against the glass, causing him to jump back in alarm. Someone was down below, trying to attract his attention! Heart racing, he groped for the catch and opened the window.

"Yes – who is it? What do you want?" he called in a hoarse whisper.

"It's me – Joe!" came the urgent reply, also whispered. "Can you come down, Max – it's important!"

Joe! What could he want at this time of night? Max felt the cold air from the open window wrap itself around him. 'I'll be down in a minute,' he called. Frantically, he groped for his clothes in the darkness. He mustn't waken his parents! Breathlessly, in stockinged feet, he turned the handle of his bedroom door and tiptoed outside on to the landing. All was quiet. There was sure to be a creaking floorboard somewhere, like at their previous house. Cautiously, he padded along the landing, feeling his way towards the stairs, annoyed with himself at having mislaid his torch, which he normally kept beside his bed. At last he reached the top of the stairs. Now for it! The height of the tread was slightly greater than in the London house and he came perilously near to missing his step half way down and pulled up trembling. He mustn't waken the place now!

At last he felt the cold tiles of the hall floor beneath his feet and was able to guide his steps to the kitchen door without too much difficulty. The lock was rather stiff, he realised, and noisy too. Bracing himself, he turned the latch. Click! The sound of the lock opening shattered the silence. Max stood tense, his heart thumping. The noise seemed to echo through the sleeping house. He waited, hoping against hope that he would not hear a voice or movement from above. To his relief, all remained silent.

He stepped outside into the porch. 'Joe?' he whispered. There was the crunch of footsteps on the gravel and the dim beam of a torch appeared from behind the bushes.

"Thanks for comin' down, Max," Joe said breathlessly. "Glad I got the right window. Thought you said that yours looked down on the buildin's."

"Where've you been, Joe?" Max asked in an urgent whisper. "You weren't at home when I called yesterday morning and a man accused me of snooping and told me to go away."

"That'd be our Dad," Joe replied grimly. "Th' Colonel's sacked 'im. We've got ta clear out of our cottage."

"We guessed as much," Max said. "What are you going to do? Where will you live?"

"That's what I've come about," Joe went on. "Our Dad's tryin' ta fix up for Kit an' George an' me to stay wi' Auntie Doreen up in Manchester till e' finds another job. But till then we're livin' in our Dad's cabin in th' woods."

"But why?" Max asked incredulously. "I don't understand."

Joe tried to hide his impatience. "I'll tell ya everythin' later – I promise," he said. "Right now I need your 'elp – an' quick!"

"I'll help you all I can, Joe – you know that." Max said.

"It's my moo-zeem," Joe explained. "I can't take it ta Manchester – Auntie Doreen'd 'ave a fit. D' ya think ya could look after it for me – you an' Jenny – till our Dad gets a new job?"

"But of course – of course we can!" Max exclaimed. "We'd be only too glad to."

"Thing is – we'll need ta move it down 'ere now – straight away – while our Dad's asleep," Joe went on.

"Now?" Max repeated in amazement.

"Yeh. Our Dad 'll kill me if 'e finds out I've come." Joe's voice faltered as he stifled a sob. "I'll tell ya ev'rythin' later. Please come nah – please!"

"All right, I will," Max assured him, groping around in the porch for his wellingtons. "But what about waking Jenny, there's an awful lot to carry." They decided that Jenny's help would speed the operation considerably and Max, with the faint beam of Joe's torch to guide him, tiptoed back upstairs to his sister's bedroom. As he turned the door handle, he realised the risk he was taking. What if Jenny called out, screamed even, and woke his parents? Oh well, he'd simply have to chance it. He moved noiselessly towards the bed.

"Jenny!" he whispered, bending over the still, slumbering form. "It's me – Max. Wake up!"

"Ugh?" came a sleepy mutter from the pillow.

"Joe's downstairs. He needs our help – quickly!" Max urged.

The bed creaked and Jenny sat up, startled and scarcely yet awake. "Joe – now? But – it's the middle of the night!"

"I know, but it's urgent! Please dress and come downstairs." Max pleaded.

Jenny reached for her torch on the bedside table. "All right. I'll get dressed. Be down in a minute."

Max tiptoed stealthily back downstairs to Joe. "She's coming," he whispered. "I'll get her wellies ready – save time."

Soon, the three children were making their way up the lane towards Keeper's Cottage. "Now – would someone mind telling me what exactly we're supposed to be doing at – " Jenny shone her torch on her watch "– ten to three in the morning?"

Joe explained at length why there was no time to lose if his precious museum was to be saved. "Our Dad says it's not safe for us ta stay at the cottage any longer, so we're livin' in 'is cabin till Auntie Doreen can 'ave us."

"But why?" Jenny demanded. "Surely that awful Colonel can't just sack you father and throw you all out at a moment's notice. He'd have to give you time to find somewhere else to go."

"It's not jus' that," Joe struggled to explain. "Our Dad thinks that 'e'll be reported for not 'avin' a proper 'ome for us to live in, an' that Kit an' George an' me'll 'ave ta go into care, or somethin'." Max and Jenny could see that their friend was fighting to hold back the tears.

"And you say you're living in the woods?" Max asked.

"In our Dad's keeper's cabin," Joe replied. "Our Dad thinks we'll be safe there till Uncle Geoff – that's Auntie Doreen's 'usband – can fetch us in 'is car."

"Let's hope that your father doesn't wake and find you gone," Jenny said as they approached the cottage.

To their relief, all was quiet as they made their way through the gate. Max, recalling his earlier encounter with the keeper, tried hard to hide the fear that began to grip him. What if − ? He shuddered at the thought of another confrontation.

Joe led the way along the path towards the sheds. "I've loaded most o' the bottles on me trolley, ready," he whispered. "An' th' other things are in plastic bags. We'll jus' about be able to manage 'em all, I reckon."

Sure enough, they were able to bring away almost all of Joe's treasured collection, leaving behind only a few cracked or broken bottles which he decided were not worth taking.

"I wonder what anyone would think if they met us now," Max puffed breathlessly as he struggled to keep a grip on a bulging fertiliser bag packed with fossils and bones.

"Glad it's downhill, anyway," said Jenny, helping Joe to steer the loaded trolley. They reached Oaklands at last, having lost only one bottle, which rolled off the trolley on the steepest stretch of the lane and disappeared into the overgrown verge. Jenny opened the gates and the boys carefully steered the trolley into the drive and parked it by the garage.

"Best not risk opening it − might wake Dad," Max said to Joe. "We'll store everything away safely tomorrow until you can come to collect them."

"Today!" Jenny corrected him. "It's nearly half past three in the morning!"

"I'd better be goin'" Joe said, " − in case our Dad misses me." He turned towards the gate. "Thanks for all ya 'elp."

"When shall we see you again?" Max whispered.

"Dunno," came the reply. "I'll try an' pop round before we go ta Manchester. Thanks again." He turned quickly and was gone.

~~~~~~~~~

Breakfast was over. Jenny and Max had just finished explaining to their parents about their early-morning adventure.

"There isn't much point in making a fuss now," Mr Davis said severely. "but you really should have wakened us. It's quite a serious matter, you see. More serious that either of you seem to understand."

"But we couldn't refuse to help Joe, could we?" Max protested.

"We didn't want to disturb you." Jenny added.

"I think we'd better tell them what Miss Keynes told us about Mr Pegler, dear," Mrs Davis said to her husband.

Their father leaned forwards towards them across the table and they could tell by his earnest manner that what he had to say was of great importance. "As you know, Mum and I learned a good deal about the various problems concerning this village yesterday," he began. "We didn't tell you everything that the headmistress told us about Mr Pegler because . . ." he paused, choosing his words carefully before continuing, ". . . because we didn't think it would be particularly helpful. However, in view of this latest little episode, we think you should know the whole truth." Again he paused, and resting his elbows on the table, looked intently into each of the children's faces in turn before continuing. "Since his wife died, Mr Pegler has become a changed man. Apparently, he was never easy to get on with, especially with grown-ups, but he has become gradually worse. He is difficult to help because he is suspicious of anyone who tries to offer assistance. He even refused Miss Keynes's offer to apply for free school meals for the children – insisted on feeding them himself."

"Yes, he was pretty horrible to me, that morning," Max

recalled unhappily.

"That'll be why he's trying to arrange for Joe and the others to stay at their relatives in Manchester," Jenny added.

"Poor man. He must feel terribly persecuted," Mrs Davis said.

The four sat in subdued silence for some time. Jenny suddenly turned to her mother. "Couldn't the children come and live with us, Mum, until Mr Pegler finds a new job? It wouldn't be for long, surely?"

Their parents exchanged glances. "We've thought about that – very hard indeed," Mrs Davis said. "But there's another problem which we haven't yet mentioned."

"Mr Pegler is not only a difficult man to deal with," Mr Davis said, "but he's also illiterate."

"You mean – he can't read – or write?" asked Jenny in amazement.

"I'm afraid not," her father replied. "Miss Keynes told us that he only got the keeper's job because no-one else wanted it. He was a local man, passionate about wild life. Didn't care about anything else, apparently."

"An illiterate person is at a terrible disadvantage in life, no matter how good he is at his job," Mrs Davis said. "He can't read advertisements for new jobs and if he could he would be unable to write applying for them."

"Someone should help him," Max exclaimed.

Mr Davis gave a helpless shrug. "Maybe. But what if someone is too proud to accept help?"

"Oh dear, what can we do?" Jenny said despairingly.

"We *must* do something," Max insisted. "Joe would be terribly unhappy in a big city like Manchester."

Mrs Davis rose from the able and rested a hand on each of the children's shoulders. "There's a home here for those children, and for as long as they need it," she said softly. "If only we can find a way of getting their father to see reason."

~~~~~~~~~

After storing away Joe's treasured collection in one of the outbuildings, the children set off down to the village to post Jenny's letter to Miss Ferriday.

"What have you said to her, apart from asking her if she wants her book back?" Max asked, throwing a sidelong glance at his sister.

"Oh – not much," Jenny answered evasively. "I just told her how unhappy the village was and asked her to help."

"How – in what way?" Max persisted.

"Just asked her, that's all." Max frowned. His sister had assumed her irritating casual manner, and he realised that no amount of questioning would persuade her to say more than she intended. They walked the rest of the way in silence.

On the way back, however, Jenny suddenly spoke. "I'm going to find Mr Pegler's cabin this afternoon. Are you coming?"

Max's jaw fell open in disbelief.

"Well – are you or aren't you?" Jenny's voice challenged.

"Of course – yes!" Max gulped.

"Good," came the reply. "but don't breathe a word to Dad

or Mum. It's a bit risky but it's the only way."

"But….. What do you . . .?" Max began.

"Wait and see," Jenny cut him short. "Come on. We mustn't be late for lunch."

Chapter 5

Accident!

They stood by the abandoned lodge at the entrance to the Hall drive. Earlier, Max had somewhat proudly pointed out to his sister the remains of Park Cottages, hidden beneath the tangled undergrowth. Jenny had dismissed his discovery with a nod, however, and he felt rather deflated. Not only that, but he was still completely in the dark about Jenny's plan. His sister really *was* impossible at times. He watched in silence as she opened the plastic bag she was carrying, took out Miss Ferriday's book, and opened out the map, which she began to study intently.

"I'm pretty sure that this is Mr Pegler's cabin," she said, pointing to a small hut-like structure in the middle of a large tract of woodland to the left of the drive. "We could have approached it from the back of Keeper's Cottage, I suppose, but I'd rather not risk meeting Mr Pegler until we find his cabin, and there's just a chance that he might be somewhere along the path."

"Surely you didn't need to bring the book," Max said. "We could have made a copy of the map – or memorised it, even. It's not ours, remember."

"It's part of my plan," Jenny responded primly.

46

Max's patience was finally exhausted. "Your plan!" he stormed. "I'm fed up with your precious plan! You get some crazy idea in your head and expect me to . . ."

"It isn't crazy – and I don't expect you to do anything!" his sister retorted hotly. "You needn't come if you don't want to – it's not too late to go back home!"

"You might need me. I've met Joe's father, remember – you haven't!" Max countered.

"And you didn't exactly end up the best of friends, did you, from what I recall," Jenny gave back witheringly.

Realising that he was getting nowhere, Max changed his approach. "I only want to know what you intend saying to Mr Pegler, and why you brought the book, that's all," he said.

Jenny responded accordingly. "All right, I'll tell you. You heard what Dad said about Mr Pegler being keen on nature . . ."

"Like Joe," Max said.

"Yes. Well, I thought that if I – we – could show him Miss Ferriday's book, and let him know that we're nature lovers too, and mean no harm, he might agree to let Joe and the others stay at Oaklands until he finds another job," Jenny explained.

Max weighed up the scheme thoughtfully. "Yes, sounds a good idea," he conceded at last. "I only hope it works, that's all."

"So do I," said Jenny. "Come on, there should be a path leading into the woods somewhere along the drive." Sure enough, they had not gone far when they noticed a narrow grassy path leading off to the left under the avenue of lime trees fringing the winding drive. "This'll be the way," Jenny said. They left the drive and followed the path, which soon emerged into a rough meadow. "Look, there's the wood – straight ahead," Jenny said, pointing confidently and striding out at a pace which caused Max, whose legs were somewhat shorter, to have to run almost to keep up with her. Eventually, they reached a thick, overgrown hedge, which they passed through over a wooden stile. Instead of leading straight on towards the woodland, as they had expected, the path now veered sharply to the right. Jenny hesitated and consulted the map.

"Funny!" she said breathlessly. "According to this, the path should lead almost in a straight line to the wood. Look!"

Max craned over to see. "I think we've taken the wrong path," he said with a frown. "This one leads to the lake – here." He pointed. "We should have kept on further along the drive and then taken the next track off to the left."

Jenny screwed up her eyes and stamped her foot impatiently. "Well, I'm not going all the way back now, that's for sure."

Max pored over the map. "We don't need to – look," he said, tracing a line with his finger. "If we follow this path for a short way, it joins up with the path we should have taken. It'll be quite straightforward then, all the way to the keeper's cabin." He pointed to the drawing of their objective.

Jenny turned away. "Oh, I can't be bothered with maps!" she snapped, her eyes on the woodland ahead. "We don't need a map, or a special path either, when the wood is right in front of us. Come on!"

"But it's a huge wood!" Max protested. "There may be

barbed wire or fallen trees or . . ."

"There's only one keeper's cabin. We're bound to find it somewhere," his sister said impulsively. "Are you coming or aren't you?"

"I suppose so", Max muttered, following reluctantly. That was Jenny all over – just wouldn't listen, no matter how patiently he explained things. Do her good, starting at that big school at Chipping Burton next week. Should bring her down a peg or two.

They soon reached the edge of the wood. There was no sign of the barbed wire that Max had feared but the perimeter of the wood was surrounded by a thick hedge.

Jenny, however, was undeterred. "We'll just keep on walking to the right," she said with a sweep of her arm. "I expect we'll come to that path you were on about soon."

Although it was a hot summer's day, the low-lying margin of the meadow was shaded from the sun and the ground was waterlogged in places. The children tried to pick their way at first, using the occasional tufts of dry grass as stepping stones, but first Max, then Jenny, missed a foothold and they resigned themselves to getting their feet wet. Soon they were wading almost up to their ankles in muddy water, their progress reduced to a laboured plod and their bodies tiring rapidly.

"Look, there's a gap in the hedge!" Jenny, who was leading, suddenly exclaimed. They soon saw that a rough causeway approached the wood from the right and plunged through the hedge to vanish from view beneath the trees.

"But it's not a proper footpath . .." Max started to say.

Jenny, however, was already heading off under the trees. "Soon be there now – come on!" she called.

Full of misgivings, Max followed. Relieved to feel a firm, dry surface beneath their feet, they pressed on into the depths of the wood. Giant sycamore trees rose up like massive church pillars on either side, their mighty boughs branching to form an almost continuous leafy arch overhead. Between the trees they could see a dense tangle of shrubs and low vegetation stretching away in all directions. After a time, the tall trees began to thin out, to be replaced by a straggling assortment of smaller trees, chiefly ash and birch, interspersed with occasional clumps of fir, with the gaps between filled by dense patches of scrubby thorn bushes.

They had been vaguely aware of the continuous drone of flies above their heads since first entering the wood but had given little thought to the matter. Suddenly, however, they were assailed by biting and stinging insects from every direction. Clouds of tiny midges descended, as though by magic signal, to torment their eyes, ears, noses, to infest their hair, and even to get inside their clothing. Max tried counter-attacking with a leafy branch he broke from a bush but soon he gave up in despair and fatigue.

They plodded on grimly, following the track, which veered sharply to the left and started to climb. The trees now began to thin out, leaving only patches of scrub. Max stopped, puzzled.

We seem to be leaving the wood,' he said. "We must be going in the wrong direction." Jenny pulled up impatiently. "Well, at least the flies have gone," she replied, taking a comb from the pocket of her jeans and attempting to tidy her tangled hair.

Max consulted the map. "Yes, I can see where we went wrong," he said despondently. "We should have kept on along the edge of the wood for a short distance further and then turned . . . ”

“What? Through more of that muddy water – no thanks!” Jenny interrupted. “I'd rather face an extra mile of walking – and the flies – rather than endure that. Come on, you're supposed to be the navigator. Which way do we go now?”

“There's no choice, really,” came the weary reply. “Either we turn back or we just keep plodding on.” He studied the map intently. “According to this, we shall soon come to a sort of hollow and there appears to be a path of some kind leading round the edge of it and back into the wood.”

Jenny replaced her comb. “Well, I'm certainly not going back. Let's try the path by the hollow. Come on!”

As Max had predicted, the track soon began to dip sharply between a few stunted trees and plunged into a steep-sided hollow, littered with overgrown heaps of rubble, from which small bushes and saplings sprouted. Max looked up at the exposed rock face rising sheer before them. His keen eye spotted a pair of jackdaws perched on a high ledge, their plumage glinting a rich purple-black against the cream-coloured rock. “Just as I thought – it's a quarry,” he panted. “All the buildings for miles around would have been built of stone from here. Been abandoned for years, by the look of it.”

Jenny too looked up, shielding her eyes from the sun. “Where's the path you were on about? I can't see any sign of it.”

Once again, Max pored over the map. “It should start just over there.” He pointed to a gap in the bushes, not far from where they stood.

Jenny set off in the direction he indicated. “Yes, you're

right!" she called from between the bushes. "There is a sort of path – come on!"

Max joined her and they began to ascend the narrow, indistinct path, which climbed tortuously through the overgrown vegetation along the edge of the quarry. Bramble bushes grew in profusion by the path and the first luscious blackberries were just ripening, tempting the children to feast on them as they climbed. The further they progressed, however, the less distinct the path became and soon they had to fight their way through a dense tangle of roots, brambles and thorny branches, with the wood still a depressing distance ahead.

Max, hot and breathless with the effort, paused once again to take another look at the map. He had studied this particular area so often and with such care that he felt he knew every detail. Miss Ferriday had certainly gone to a great deal of trouble to ensure its accuracy. Even so, sixty-odd years was an awfully long time. Suppose the path had been abandoned, like everything else around Tangleton seemed to be? The going was almost impossible now – what if it got worse? Supposing they . . .

"Max, quick – I'm falling! Help!"

His speculations were cut short as Jenny's cry of alarm, accompanied by a frantic scraping sound, came from the overgrown path ahead. He dropped the book and scrambled wildly in the direction from which the sounds had come. Reaching the place where Jenny had been standing, he pulled up in alarm. His sister had disappeared.

He stood horrorstruck. "Jenny!" he called. He heard his own voice, half-strangled with fear, call out, "Jenny – where are you?" There was no reply. Desperate by now, he looked in vain from left to right before the truth finally dawned – the quarry! She had fallen down the sheer rock face into the old quarry! Trembling, he groped his way towards the edge. Yes, there was a gap in the bushes. She must have pushed through, lost her balance, and – he felt sick at the thought. What could he do? He stood for a moment, paralysed, incapable of movement, rooted to the spot. He had to do something, though what, he had no idea.

Willing himself into action at last, he sank down on his hands and knees and forcing himself to ignore the thorns and briars that tore at his skin, crawled to the quarry edge. At last, parting the fringe of spiky grasses clinging to the rim of the rock face, he peered down. "Jenny – are you there?" he called through parched lips. His voice echoed back eerily from the depths of the quarry. No reply. He strained his eyes in the hope of spotting some sign. At first he could see nothing except for the tops of the bushes on the quarry floor, a frightening distance below. But then, slightly to the left, his eye came to rest on a protruding ledge of rock, some twenty feet or so below where he knelt. His heart raced as he picked out the unmistakable colour of Jenny's jeans, partly hidden by the foliage of the bushes.

"Jenny – I can see you!" he called, "Are you all right?" Straining to catch a reply, he thought he heard a faint groan. He leaned further over and cupped his hands so that his words would carry better. "Don't try to move, I'm going to fetch help – I'll not be long."

Edging his way back from the quarry rim, he looked desperately around. He couldn't possibly reach his sister without help, of that he was certain. He had to get help quickly – but how? Retrace his steps all the way back home to get Dad? Dismay filled his mind at the thought. Yet what was the alternative? There was none – except for stumbling on in the vain hope of finding Mr Pegler's cabin, somewhere in the huge expanse of woodland. His mind raced. Frantically, he dragged the largest of several rotting branches lying nearby to the edge of the quarry and fixed it upright in a thorn bush to guide him back to the spot. Now – which way? He could delay the decision no longer. The keeper's cabin was nearer – it had to be – but it would be safer to fetch Dad.

He had just begun the laborious descent back the way they had come when he pulled up abruptly. The report of a gunshot echoed from the woods, shattering the silence and causing an alarmed woodpigeon to rise into the air with a clatter. Mr Pegler! Again, Max hesitated. Should he – dare he – try to find the keeper? He stood in an agony of indecision, utterly at a loss what to do, trying to weight up the best course of action, yet unable to think clearly.

Crack! Another shot, this time nearer, resolved the matter. Yes, he would press on in the hope of finding Mr Pegler. Surely he would help when he knew what had happened. Fired with fresh determination, Max turned and battled on up the overgrown path, paying no heed to the treacherous web of roots and branches that snared him and tore at his clothes. He had to find the keeper. Jenny's life depended on it.

At last, fighting for breath, his hands scratched and bleeding and his clothes torn, he reached the wood. Scrambling thankfully over the fence, he struck off under the trees, searching for a path and aiming as best he could in the direction from which the shots had come. The trees were firs, standing in tightly-packed rows, their canopy shutting out the light almost completely. Max stumbled on over the dark, barren ground. If only he could find a path or better still, hear another gunshot! Eventually he came to a firebreak between the rows of firs. It was a relief to feel grass beneath his feet and he broke into a staggering run. The trees on either side began to thin out. Piles of sawn timber lay on the cleared ground and conical heaps of wood-ash at intervals indicated that the branches from the fir poles had been burnt there recently.

He pulled up, breathless. 'Mr Pegler – help!' he called. His voice rang through the trees. His ears strained in vain for a reply. Silence. Weary in body and spirit, he staggered on. A clump of large, broadleaved trees appeared before him and to his relief, he reached a clearly-defined path, which crossed the grassy ride at right angles. After a moment's hesitation he plunged right along the path, which skirted a cluster of knobbly old oaks whose branches reached out to form a leafy canopy overhead.

Suddenly, from only a short distance in front, there was a frantic clatter of wings and an ear-shattering cry of alarm as a cock pheasant hurtled away between the trees. Max hurried on, his taut nerves jangled still further, his body aching almost to the point of collapse. Then, like a mirage ahead, a low wooden building with a thatched roof came into view through the trees. The cabin! Max forced himself into a lurching run. The cabin was nearer now, almost within hailing distance. A few more yards and he would . . .

The thought died abruptly as he felt himself brought to a standstill by a vice-like grip on his shoulder.

Chapter 6

The Rescue

Max found himself being spun round to face his captor. Mr Pegler, in shirtsleeves, though still wearing Wellingtons and carrying his gun, looked down at him with a cold, hostile stare.

"You again!" he hissed through his bristly beard, his iron grip showing no sign of relaxing. "Thought I told ya ta keep away from 'ere."

Max's desperation gave him fresh courage. "Mr Pegler, come quickly – there's been an accident!" The words erupted with a rush, stinging the keeper with their impact.

"An' who d' yer think you're orderin' about?" he snapped. "I've told yer before, I'll not 'ave yer snoopin' about an' trespassin'. Nah clear off th' way yer came – an' quick!"

"But it's Jenny – my sister – Joe's friend!" Max blurted, close to tears. "She's fallen down the quarry! Please come quickly – please!"

Mr Pegler stiffened attentively. Max felt the grip on his

shoulder ease slightly. "Quarry? What quarry?"

Max pointed wildly in the direction from which he had come. "The big quarry. Over beyond the wood. The one with trees –"

"What were you doin', playin' there?" Mr Pegler demanded. "Want yer 'eads examinin' – an' yer parents for lettin' yer."

"We weren't playing – and our parents don't know we're here," Max went on hysterically. "We were looking for you. My sister wanted to show you something. We got lost. Please help!"

The keeper released his grip and stood motionless, deep in thought. Max began to describe what had happened, trying to get the man to understand the urgency of the situation. Suddenly he noticed a figure approaching from the direction of the cabin. It was Joe.

"Max! What are you doin' 'ere – an' where's Jenny?" Joe gasped in surprise.

Max turned to him. "She's fallen down the quarry on to a ledge. She's trapped. I think she's alive – she groaned. She . . ."

"Shut up you two, an' listen!" Mr Pegler cut them short. "Joe, slip back to th' cabin an' get my axe – an' that coil o' rope from behind th' door. Tell Kit ta stay wi' George. We may be gone quite a while, tell 'er." Joe needed no second bidding. He was back off towards the cabin in an instant.

Mr Pegler turned to Max. "Fell down th' old quarry, eh?"

Max nodded, trying to hold back the tears. "We were climbing the path by the quarry side. We were about half way up. Suddenly Jenny slipped . . ."

"Mad, yer must 'ave been – mad!" the keeper snarled. "That

path's not been used for years! Even I wouldn't risk climbin' it. Come on!" He turned abruptly and set off with long raking strides in the direction of the quarry with Max, tired and breathless, endeavouring to keep up with him. Soon Joe, carrying a huge axe and with a coil of thick rope round his shoulders, caught him up.

Instead of turning off along the way Max had come, Mr Pegler followed the track until they came to the edge of the fir plantation. Climbing the fence, Max realised that the keeper was taking a quicker, more direct route. Soon the path began to dip and Max recognised the rough sloping ground over which he had scrambled a short time before. "Over there – where that branch is pointing!" he called out breathlessly. "That's where she fell!"

Mr Pegler struck off without hesitation up the treacherous overgrown rim of the quarry, with the two boys struggling desperately to keep up with him.. Max, utterly spent by now, tripped headlong over a tangle of briars, scratching his face painfully. Joe helped him to his feet and sensing his friend's state, assisted him along the last difficult stretch of ground. "Our Dad 'll save 'er, Max – if anybody can," he said.

Mr Pegler got down on all fours and crawled to the quarry edge. "Got summat blue on, 'as she?" he demanded, peering down intently.

"Yes – blue jeans," Max stammered.

Mr Pegler grunted. "Thought as much. It's a 'ell of a way down there." Wriggling nearer the edge, he craned over. "Listen, kid," he called, his voice softer than before, "I'm goin' ta try ta get down ta ya," adding under his breath "though 'eaven knows 'ow." Raising his voice once more, he called "Lie still, kid, an' don't try ta move – okay? It may take some time but jus' do as I tell ya. Understand?"

"Y- yes," came a tearful response from below. Max breathed a sigh of relief.

Mr Pegler crawled back from the edge and rose to his feet. "Talk about luck!" he said, uncoiling the rope. "If she'd fallen a couple o' yards on either side, she'd 'ave been a gonner – wouldn't 'ave stood a chance." He looked round for something firm to which to fasten the rope. The nearest sizeable tree was some distance away. The rope would not be long enough.

"Come wi' me," he ordered the two boys. They followed him to the nearest clump of trees, where with a few lusty swings of his axe he cut a number of strong stakes. These he sharpened to a point at one end and told Max and Joe to carry them back to the quarry edge. Then, choosing a suitable spot as near to the edge as possible, and using the axe as a pick, he scooped out a hole in the ground, into which he drove the stakes with the blunt end of the axe. After scraping back the soil into the hole, firming it with his feet and satisfying himself that the stakes were securely fixed, he knotted one end of the rope round them.

"Couple o' things we've got ter find out now," he said, wiping his mouth with the back of his hand. "Is th' rope long enough, an' are you two young 'uns strong enough ter pull me back up?" He played out the rope over the edge and again lying flat, peered over. By craning his neck, Max could just see the end of the rope dangled well below where Jenny lay.

"So far so good," Mr Pegler muttered, hauling back the rope. "Nah comes th' tricky bit – can you two hold my weight?" Sitting down behind the stakes, to which he had fastened the rope, he showed the boys exactly what they had to do. Then, after tying the other end of the rope round his waist, he slowly lowered himself over the edge until his feet were resting on a narrow ledge jutting out a few feet below.

"Right – pull!" he shouted. The boys gripped the rope and pulled as hard as they could. Max, still weary from his recent ordeal, realised to his dismay that his efforts were in vain and that Joe was having to heave with all his might to make up for his own miserable attempt. At last Mr Pegler's head appeared above the edge and he scrambled back on to the firm ground.

"Well, that's no good," he gasped, "You couldn't even pull me up from jus' over th' edge. 'ad to 'aul myself up." He displayed his hands, the palms of which were red and sore from the effort.

"What about me goin' down, Dad?" Joe suggested. "I'm a lot lighter than you, an' you an' you an' Max could pull me up easily."

Mr Pegler looked at his son doubtfully. "I'd wondered 'bout that, Joe," he said. "It'll be rough goin', mind – steerin' yourself wi' your feet. Then when ya reach th' ledge, it'll mean takin' th' rope off an' fastenin' it round th' lass, then tellin' 'er what ta do."

"I could do it, Dad," Joe insisted. "I know I could. Let me – please!"

Max could tell that Mr Pegler was far from convinced. "Let's see if ya can manage th' knots," he said at last. Joe sat down and they practised knotting and untying the rope around his waist. At last the keeper seemed reasonably satisfied.

"You'll let me do it, won't ya, Dad?" Joe pleaded. "I know what ta do now – honest!"

"She may be 'urt, mind," his father warned. "If she's 'urt

bad, you'll 'ave to stay with 'er till we fetch 'elp from th' village."

"I unnerstand, Dad." Joe assured him.

Mr Pegler gave way at last. Joe checked the rope and crawled to the quarry edge.

"Take it slow an' careful," his father stressed as he and Max prepared to play out the rope. "An' shout if ya 'ave any trouble an' we'll pull ya up straight away."

Joe disappeared gradually out of view. Max, although doing his best to help, was aware that Mr Pegler was bearing the brunt of the weight. Even so, he gripped the rope determinedly as Joe was lowered down the rock face, wincing as the moving rope burnt his hands as it slowly uncoiled.

"Steady – I'm nearly there!" Joe called. Mr Pegler, sweating with the effort, slowed down the rate of descent until the rope suddenly slackened. Joe had reached the ledge.

"Okay!" came the voice from below. They put down the rope and crawled to the edge. Joe had undone the knot from round his waist and they watched as he eased his way to where Jenny lay. Max could hear Joe talking quietly to his sister but it was impossible to catch what he was saying.

" 'ow is she, Joe?" Mr Pegler called down.

"Seems all right – 'cept for 'er ankle an' 'er wrist," came the reply. "Says they 'urt – might be broke, even."

Mr Pegler frowned. "Take ya time, Joe," he called. "Check that rope carefully." He turned to Max. "I'll draw 'er up," he said. "You wait 'ere an' 'elp 'er when she's within grabbin' distance."

"Right Dad – we're ready!" Joe called.

Mr Pegler sat down behind the stakes to which the rope was tied, and braced himself. "Watch that rope over th' edge," he ordered Max, "an' tell me if it gets caught on anythin'. Right, Joe," he called, "I'm pullin' 'er up!" Grimly, hand over hand, the keeper hauled in the rope. Max peered anxiously over the edge, watching intently as Jenny was slowly lifted upwards, her pale frightened face looking up pleadingly towards him.

"Well done, Jenny," Max whispered. "You're doing fine. It won't be long now."

Beads of sweat stood out on Mr Pegler's brow. His face was a mask of concentration. The muscled of his bare arms stood out like rigid cords as he drew Jenny inch by inch to safety. Suddenly Max noticed with alarm that Jenny's weight was causing the rope to cut deeply into the stony soil as it passed over the edge. Supposing it became worn through! There was still Joe to come up when his sister had been rescued. He told Mr Pegler of his fears.

"Can't do anythin' 'bout it now," the keeper gasped between clenched teeth. "We'll slide a stake under it before we pull Joe up." To Max's relief, Jenny was by now almost within reach. As he leaned over, waiting to help her over the edge, he could see her face clearly for the first time. Scratched and bruised, her eyes red from crying, she looked a pitiful sight. Yet this was the same wilful, confident sister with whom he had set off from home only a few hours previously! "I can almost reach her!" he called to Mr Pegler. He heard the keeper grunt with a final effort and thankfully grasped Jenny's hands and helped her on to the firm ground. Mr Pegler crawled over to where they lay and untied the rope from around Jenny's waist.

" 'ow ya feelin', lass?" he asked anxiously.

"A bit better now – thanks," Jenny whispered, wincing with pain, "except for my ankle and my wrist. They both hurt. I don't think I could stand."

Mr Pegler began examining the rope, ready for lowering it to Joe. "You jus' lie there, an' take it easy for a while," he said. "An' if ya can't walk, then this brother o' yours 'll 'ave ta carry ya." To Max's amazement, the keeper gave him a solemn yet unmistakable wink.

Max got to his feet. "I'll just get another stake for the rope to run over – like you said," he called, picking up the axe and heading towards the clump of trees.

"Aye, good lad," Mr Pegler said. "Th' rope's standin' up to th' strain very well but a stake 'll make th' pullin' easier."

While Max slowly and laboriously cut and trimmed a suitable stake, Mr Pegler leaned over the quarry edge to make sure that Joe was ready. Then, with Max's stake in position, they lowered the rope once more.

"Right Max – I'm ready," Joe called. Again, Max watched anxiously as the slow process got under way, this time bringing his friend to safety. Soon he was able to reach over and help Joe back on to safe ground. The pair of them sat for some time, exhausted by their efforts.

Despite her discomfort, Jenny had by now recovered sufficiently to thank the Peglers for saving her life. "I think you're both heroes," she said solemnly. "and I'm sure Mum and Dad will think so too."

Joe turned towards Max. "But we couldn't have rescued ya if it 'adn't been for Max."

"Thank you too, Max," Jenny added.

Mr Pegler got wearily to his feet and looked down at Jenny.

"Well, if ya can't walk, lass, there's only one thing for it." Bending down, he swept Jenny up and into his arms. "We'd best get ya ta Colonel Ferriday – 'e'll let ya folks know." They set off towards the wood.

"The book!" Jenny called out suddenly. "Where is the book I brought to show Mr Pegler?"

It took a frantic search before the boys spotted the bag containing Miss Ferriday's book, lying where Max had dropped it. Breathlessly, they hurried after the keeper.

"Sisters!" Max gasped. "They're impossible sometimes!"

"I know," Joe blinked. "I've got one as well, remember."

Chapter 7

The Colonel

The Hall came into view as they emerged from the wood, its ancient stonework giving off a warm, golden glow in the late-afternoon sunshine. Jenny, who had been carried along in the keeper's arms at first, now sat astride his shoulders and despite her painful ankle and wrist, her keen eyes took in every detail of the imposing building. Mr Pegler became increasingly uneasy as they drew near. Suddenly, as though unaware that Joe was still with them, he wheeled round.

"Get back ta th' cabin, Joe – quick!" he snapped. "Ya' know I've told ya ta keep away from this place! Your job's ta look after Kit an' George. Nah off ya go – sharp!"

Joe, eyes downcast, turned away.

"Thank you, Joe – you were very brave." Jenny said.

Max threw his friend a meaningful glance. "Hope to see you again before – before you – before very long," he whispered.

Joe plodded forlornly back the way they had come, while the others made their way round the back of the great building to a small side doorway.

"Ring th' bell," Mr Pegler ordered Max. After a short wait the door opened and a small grey-haired lady with bright eyes set in a rosy-cheeked, dimpled face stood looking up at them enquiringly.

"This kid fell down th' quarry – them new folks at Oaklands," the keeper blurted.

The lady was obviously taken aback. "Oh, er, well – you'd better bring her inside, Mr Pegler – through here." She led the way into a large room with a high beamed ceiling. Mr Pegler lowered Jenny into a chair. "Says she can't walk – 'er ankle or summat", he said thickly, straightening up. "I'd better be off – no time ta 'ang about." He turned abruptly towards the door and was gone.

"The book!" Jenny exclaimed. "You forgot to give him the book! Go after him. Tell him he can borrow it and return it later. Try to get him to – you know!" she added, giving Max a meaningful glance.

Stepping through the door, Max could see the keeper striding out purposefully back down the drive towards the woods. He hesitated. Better not shout – Mr Pegler might take offence. Or ignore him completely, even. He always seemed to get landed with the difficult situations. Oh, well, there was only one thing to do. Gripping the bag tightly, he set off in pursuit of the rapidly disappearing keeper. At last, breathless from running, he drew abreast of the striding man.

"Mr Pegler!" he stammered, "Jenny – my sister – says please would you look at this book and – and – let her have it back when – when – you've finished with it. Oh, and . . ."

"Book? What book?" the keeper snapped. "I've no time for books. I – I don't read 'em."

Max suddenly recalled what the schoolmistress had told

his parents. "But it's not just reading, Mr Pegler," he tried to explain. "There are nature pictures too – animals, birds, butterflies. They're good pictures. Perhaps you'd show them to Joe – please!"

Mr Pegler slowed down slightly. "Nature, ya say?" he mumbled.

"Yes!" Max was quick to assure him. "Birds, especially. They're the best bird pictures I've ever seen – woodpeckers, owls, nightjars –"

"I'll 'ave a look at it an' send it back wi' Joe," Mr Pegler replied briefly, snatching the bag awkwardly from Max's hand.

"Thanks very much, Mr Pegler for – for everything." Max called as the keeper strode off under the trees.

He could hear his sister's voice mingling with two adult voices as he tiptoed self-consciously back into the Hall. How right Dad had been when he remarked that Jenny bounced back from every disaster like a rubber ball against a wall!

"Yes, here's Max, Colonel Ferriday," Jenny announced from her chair as he entered the room. Max found himself looking up into the face of a tall, lean elderly gentleman, with silvery hair and moustache, dressed in a khaki-coloured jersey, faded corduroy trousers, and sandals on his feet.

"Ah, so you're our young lady's brother," the man said, advancing towards Max with outstretched hand. Max extended his own hand diffidently, and winced as the Colonel took it in a vice-like grip and pumped it solemnly

"I'm afraid that we have something of a problem, er – Max," the Colonel said. "Your sister tells me that your telephone is not yet connected, which means that we cannot contact your parents direct." He gave a slight nervous cough.

"Unfortunately, Mr Hicks, my butler, has taken the car into Chipping Burton. We seem to have no alternative, therefore, but to wait until he returns, which may be a little while yet."

"I'll be all right," Jenny assured him.

The Colonel turned to his housekeeper. "How severe are the injuries, Mrs Bannister?" he asked.

The lady bent forward and examined Jenny's ankle, which, Max noticed, was wrapped in a wet towel, as was her left wrist. "Sprains, I'd say – perhaps breaks, even. Certainly cases for a doctor, sir," she replied.

Although their mother had registered the family with a doctor at Chipping Burton, the children were unable to recall his name. The Colonel paced up and down the room, humming tunelessly under his breath. Suddenly he turned once more to his housekeeper.

"Perhaps you would be good enough to watch out for Mr Hicks, Mrs Bannister," he said, stroking his moustache. "Please tell him that we shall require the car again before it is garaged."

"Very good, sir," the housekeeper said as she went out of the room.

The Colonel's restlessness made Max feel ill at ease. Jenny, however, seemed not to notice, asking questions at intervals so that the Colonel could not evade speaking. To his surprise, Max realised that instead of irritating the old gentleman, his sister's insistent manner seemed to have the opposite effect and in time the Colonel sat down and appeared to be listening intently to what she was saying.

After giving a dramatic account of her fall and eventual rescue, Jenny went on to describe their life in the city and their recent move to Tangleton. Max noticed the Colonel twitch slightly as she mentioned Oaklands.

"It's a wonderful old place!" Jenny declared enthusiastically. "Mum and Dad love it. They always wanted to live in the country – Dad especially. He became quite ill when we lived in the city. The doctor said he needed to change his job – too much worry." She gave the Colonel one of her challenging looks. "I think that country people are very lucky. Don't you?"

The old gentleman cleared his throat. "Er – yes," he replied, somewhat uncomfortably,

"They – that is, we – are most fortunate. I agree."

Max stared at his sister with alarm as she went on:

"We were very lucky to get Oaklands, you know, really. A dear old lady lived there, all alone. I expect you know. People say that she was very fond of children. I think she wanted us to live there after she'd gone." The Colonel seemed about to say something but Jenny swept on: "She loved nature too – flowers, trees, birds, butterflies. She was a marvellous artist. She painted a whole book full of lovely pictures. I found it in the garage, hidden away in a box of old rubbish. I've written to ask her if she'd like it back."

The Colonel leaned forward attentively. "Oh, really?"

"I've lent it to Mr Pegler. He loves nature too," Jenny went on. "Would you like to see it, too? I don't suppose Miss Ferriday would mind."

The Colonel cleared his throat once more.

"The – the lady you speak of – er, Miss Ferriday – is in fact, my sister," the Colonel began hesitantly. "She and . . ." He paused, his head bowed, before continuing in a faltering voice, "She and I were – very dear to one another. She lived here – at the Hall, then. She used to spend hours watching wild creatures. Drawing and painting." Again he paused before continuing with some difficulty: "Yes, the book you mention. Yes, I seem to recall it....... all those years ago. It was, as you so rightly say, an exquisite collection of paintings – yes." His voice by now was reduced to little more than a whisper and Max had to lean forward to catch the remaining words.

"They were happy days. . . very happy days." The words trailed away. There was silence.

Jenny spoke at last, also in a whisper. "But – why did she leave?" Both children waited breathlessly for a reply. For the first time, Max became aware of the measured tick of an old clock in a rosewood case on a low shelf in a corner of the room.

"She left," the Colonel answered at last, " – because we quarrelled." Again there was a pause. Suddenly he looked up, fixing his dark, moist eyes on Jenny's face. "We quarrelled over the very matter you have just mentioned, young lady," he said, his voice rising with emotion. " – my sister's love of wild things. It was entirely my fault. I was wrong – utterly wrong. I realised that later – too late." He rose and stood looking absently through the window towards the sweep of the distant woods.

"But you love nature too – you must do," Jenny said, still in hushed tones. "Living here, with all these lovely woods and fields."

The Colonel remained motionless, staring through the window. When at last he spoke, his voice had a strange, distant-sounding quality that held the children in its spell. "Yes, I love it passionately. I used to think I loved it then, all those years ago, but in a different way from Rachel, my sister. I was a hunting man in those days – and a good shot, too. The coun-

70

tryside was my playground. I lived for the thrill of the chase and the stalking of the prey." He sighed. "It hurt Rachel deeply. It was not until later that I came to realise just how deeply it hurt her."

Jenny's face puckered as she tried to understand the old gentleman's meaning. "And you say that your love of the countryside has changed?"

"Oh yes, indeed!" He turned towards them, his eyes shining with a fervour they had never before seen. "I've come to love the countryside in an entirely different way. Trying to make amends for the folly of my youth, I suppose. There will be no more cruelty on this estate – not while I live, anyway. No hunting, no shooting, no trapping – no angling, even. I am giving it all back to the wild!" He patted Jenny lightly on the head, adding in little more than a whisper, "I'd like my sister to know that. I feel certain she would approve. She might even begin to forgive me."

There was a tap on the door and Mrs Bannister entered. "Mr Hicks is back, sir," she announced.

With effort the Colonel managed to regain his composure. "Thank you, Mrs Bannister. I'd like you to accompany our young lady and her brother down to Oaklands. Her parents are sure to demand an explanation of what has occurred."

Mr Hicks carried Jenny out to the car and the Colonel tottered slowly behind to see them off.

"Drive very carefully, Hicks," he said as the car was about to leave. "Our young lady is in a fair amount of pain." He bent low to speak to Jenny through the open window. "Goodbye, my dear. I did so enjoy your company. Some other time, perhaps." A thought suddenly struck him. "Oh, er – the book. Much as I would dearly love to see it again, perhaps in the circumstances, I had better not. Rachel – Miss Ferriday – might not wish it." He sighed. "Again, some other time perhaps. Goodbye."

The car moved off, and the children waved as the old gentleman turned slowly back towards the Hall.

Chapter 8

Schemes and Surprises

Jenny lay in bed in Chipping Burton Cottage Hospital, both her badly sprained ankle and wrist encased in plaster. The doctor who had examined her had found no other injuries, but she was to stay in hospital for a few days for observation before being allowed home. A week of the summer holidays remained and it had been agreed that her father should contact her new school to find out if she could attend from the first day, using crutches.

The hospital proved to be a small, friendly place. There were only two other children sharing her ward, both younger than herself, and Jenny was soon on good terms with the nurses. Max and her parents were able to visit every afternoon, bringing news of what went on around Oaklands. Luckily, her right hand had escaped injury and she was able to spend the mornings sketching, making jottings in an exercise book in preparation for a story she intended writing and illustrating about their new life in the country, as well as reading. She also gave much thought to the future of Tangleton generally, and especially to the Pegler family.

Try as she would, she found the Colonel's behaviour impossible to understand. How could a man who had been so kind to her, and who seemed to care so passionately about wild life, allow a whole village to wither and die? Even worse, how could he treat the Peglers so badly? It just didn't make sense. And no matter how odd Miss Ferriday might be, surely she wouldn't want the estate to be allowed to go wild, if it meant families like the Peglers losing their homes. She found herself half-regretting having sent her letter to Miss Ferriday. If she had known then what she knew now, she would have made her plea to the old lady far more forceful. She could write again, of course, but she decided it would be best to await a reply to her first letter.

She lay in bed, her jaws clamped tight in concentration. Would a direct appeal to the Colonel stand more chance of success? After all, she did owe him a letter of thanks and that would provide a perfect excuse for writing! She had been quick to notice his reaction to her account of how they had come to live at Oaklands. And there was no mistaking his affection for his sister, despite their quarrel all those years ago. All this suggested that he was really a sensitive person. Yes – that was what she must do. But she would need to choose her words very carefully. She picked up her pen and writing pad, her mind made up. She would act now. There was no time to lose.

An hour or so later, after a second critical reading of what she had written, Jenny sealed the envelope and lay back against the pillow with satisfaction. After thanking Colonel Ferriday for his kindness, she had pleaded with him to reconsider his decision to dismiss Mr Pegler. She could do no more. And if the worst happened, and the old gentleman refused, she could still try to persuade Mr Pegler to allow his children to stay at Oaklands until he found another post. After all, thanks to her fall, they knew one another now and despite his odd manner, he could be worked on, she was convinced of that. And his acceptance of her offer to him of the loan of Miss Ferriday's book, – surely that all helped to build trust between them. When he returned the book, she would send him some of her best nature sketches – to keep. 'I just hope that Joe and the others aren't whisked off to Manchester before then,' she said aloud.

~~~~~~~~

"I was faced with a problem," said Mr Davis, sitting with his wife and Max by Jenny's bedside. "Mum and I wanted to express our gratitude to Mr Pegler and Joe – and also to Colonel Ferriday for his help in the affair. I knew that I could write to the Colonel, or telephone him from the call box in the village, but that it would be no use writing to Mr Pegler. So I decided to go and see the Colonel, hoping that I might come across Mr Pegler by accident." He chuckled as he recalled what had happened. "The Colonel was very charming – not at all what I had expected. He was most concerned about you, Jenny – referred to you as 'Our young lady!'"

Jenny, propped up in bed, listened eagerly to every word. "Yes, I admit he was very nice," she reflected. "He even said that he'd enjoyed my company."

Max grimaced. "He hasn't had to put up with it for very long, that's why!" he said with feeling. "Oaklands is as quiet now as it was when Miss Ferriday lived there!"

Jenny was quick to respond. "I bet it's not as quiet as our other house was when you were away at cub camp!" she retorted.

Mrs Davis laughed. "Well, it's good to see that you two have lost none of your mutual affection, anyway."

Jenny was eager to hear more about her father's visit to the Hall.

"Well, the Colonel was very keen to know when you leave hospital," Mr Davis continued. "He asked to be kept informed of your progress."

"I've written to thank him for being so kind," said Jenny, adding guardedly, "I only wish he'd be kind to the Peglers too."

"Which brings me to the next stage of my story," Mr Davis said. "I was just walking back along the Hall drive when a boy appeared from a path out of the woods . . ."

"Joe!" Jenny and Max exclaimed together.

"I knew from your description that it must be your friend," Mr Davis said, "so I introduced myself and thanked him for what he had done. He said that he was on his way to Oaklands to return the book and he told me that his father was at the keeper's cabin so I took a chance and went back with him. Mr Pegler was very suspicious at first. Even accused me of being a snooper from the council! But gradually I got across who I was and why I had come . . ."

"Did you ask him if Joe and the others could come and stay at Oaklands?" Jenny demanded.

Her father raised a calming hand. "I couldn't, Jenny – not just then. You can't rush things with a man like Mr Pegler. But I will next time I see him. I promise."

"At least he knows Dad now," Mrs Davis reminded Jenny. "These things have to be done gradually. We thought that when you come out of hospital, Jenny, we could invite Joe to tea and think up some way of persuading his father to call on us too."

"Let's hope it's not too late," Jenny said. "They may be swept off to Manchester any day."

Mrs Davis whispered something to Max, who rummaged in a bag he was carrying and took out two small parcels, wrapped in crumpled brown paper. "This is from Joe", he said, handing a long, slender package to his sister.

Jenny tore open the wrapper with her free hand and held up the contents in delight. It consisted of an arrangement of pheasant feathers set into a carefully-polished block of wood. "Isn't it lovely!" Jenny beamed. "All the trouble he must have gone to!"

"'And Mr Pegler sent you this," said Max, passing his sister the second package. They all watched as one-handed she gingerly opened the wrapper and joined in her astonishment as a delicately-carved bird was revealed.

"A great spotted woodpecker!" Max gasped. " – and just look at the detail – it must have taken him hours to carve."

"Mr Pegler's a true craftsman – there's no doubt about it," Mr Davis said, turning the carving over slowly in his hands.

"They're both lovely presents," Mrs Davis added. "Joe seems to have inherited his father's artistic gift."

By now, Jenny was finding it difficult to keep her emotions in check. "We must help them – we must!" she urged, close to tears.

On their visit to the hospital the following day, Max and his parents had two more surprises for Jenny. The first was a bouquet of flowers from the Colonel, with an accompanying card bearing the message: "Get well soon, young lady. Every good wish. Claude Ferriday."

The second surprise was a letter, addressed in slightly wavering yet distinctive handwriting, and bearing a Chipping Burton postmark.

"Miss Ferriday!" exclaimed Jenny excitedly. "She's replied! I wonder what she says?"

"Open it and find out," Max suggested.

Jenny hesitated. "I want to, of course, but . . ."

Her mother laughed. "I sense somehow that she wants to read it to herself, alone. Am I right, Jenny?"

Jenny nodded . "It's not that it's terribly secret, or anything like that," she said, for once not really sure of herself. " – and I'll tell you all about it later – read it to you, in fact."

Mr Davis winked across at Max. "Oh, don't worry, young lady, we can take a hint. We know when we're not wanted!"

"No, no – you mustn't go. I forbid it!" Jenny exclaimed, propping Miss Ferriday's letter on her bedside table. "I'll keep it until later. There's no hurry." Nevertheless, she was secretly glad when the end of visiting time came. She reached for the letter with trembling hands, tore it open and read:

Flat 4,

Bramble Court,

Fernborough,

27ᵗʰ August.

My Dear Jenny,

Your letter came as a delightful surprise! I am so glad that you and your family like Oaklands so much. I'm afraid that both the house and garden have been very much neglected during recent years, but I have no doubt that you will all enjoy restoring the place and making it into the kind of home that you want.

It is a source of great pleasure to me that Oaklands has become the home of young people. I am sure that you and your brother, together with the friends you invite home, will make Oaklands a happy place once more, as it was in former times.

Thank you very much indeed for offering to return my book on Tangleton Park. I must confess that I had completely forgotten about it. Your generous words of praise brought a blush to my cheeks! I was very keen on painting at the time, being about 18 years old, but the urge to be an artist faded soon afterwards, I'm afraid. As an aspiring artist yourself, I'm sure the book will be of far more use to you than to me, so please keep it.

It occurs to me that as you and your brother are both keen on natural history, it might be worth thinking about producing your own version of the book sometime, bringing the story of Tangleton's wild life up to the present time. I'm sure that there will be many changes to record since my book was completed.

I must confess that I have put off answering the other question that you ask until the end of my letter because quite frankly, I'm not sure how I can be of help. You say that you feel that Tangleton is a dying village, and that the people are unhappy. You are quite right, of course, on both counts. As you probably know, my brother, who is lord of the manor, has lost interest in the estate, and seems content for the people to leave and the buildings to decay. He is an old and unhappy man, and nothing I can say or do is likely to have the slightest effect on him, I'm afraid.

The only hope I can hold out is that I have been told that Ian, my brother's son, is returning shortly to assist with the running of the estate. He has only recently come back to England after living abroad for many years. What plans he will have for the estate and to what degree he will influence his father, I'm afraid I cannot say.

Oh dear, I haven't been very helpful, have I? I only wish I could be, but quite honestly I see no way out of the problem. I am keenly sorry, believe me.

Thank you once more for your charming letter, my dear. Do write again, won't you?

Sincerely yours,

Rachel Ferriday

P.S. Have you seen anything of Perkins, my cat? He ran away at the time I was preparing to leave, as though determined to remain behind at Oaklands. I do miss him. He is a large black cat with a beautiful shiny coat. I do hope that nothing terrible has happened to him.

After reading the letter a second time, Jenny slipped it back into its envelope and settled back against her pillow. Random thoughts chased one another around in her mind in a bewildering manner. It was wonderful news that she could keep the book! It would belong to the whole family, of course – it wouldn't be fair to keep it to herself. And yes – they *would* try to bring the natural history of Tangleton up to date. Max would be thrilled about that idea! And what a challenge it would be to her own artistic skill too!

Then there was the mystery of Miss Ferriday's cat. She seemed to recall Joe mentioning it at their first meeting, that morning when she and Max had climbed up the lane in the sticky heat and suddenly found themselves standing before the little cottage with the sagging roof and ramshackle sheds. Had it gone wild, as Mr Pegler, according to Joe, had predicted? Or was it still lurking around somewhere in the vicinity of Oaklands, unwilling for some reason to return to its old home? She would certainly watch out for it and try to coax it into the house so that Miss Ferriday could get it back.

But it was on the fate of the Peglers – and of Tangleton itself – that Jenny's troubled thoughts returned time and again. Why did such apparently kind, sensitive people as the Ferridays allow a quarrel that took place all those years ago spoil their

80

lives? The Colonel still cared about his sister – in fact in his wrong-headed decision to allow his estate to return to the wild, he was actually trying to please her! She reached for the letter and read the final paragraph once more. Yes – she felt sure that Miss Ferriday's words were but a thin disguise for the sisterly affection she still felt for her estranged brother.

Somehow, someone had to bring this silly quarrel to an end and save Tangleton from its fate. But who? As things stood, the only hope lay with the return of the Colonel's son. Jenny began daydreaming, a habit she had formed when faced with difficult decisions. Yes. . . it would certainly make a story-book ending. . . the handsome young hero hurrying to the rescue of the endangered village, banishing the wicked old squire and welcomed with open arms by the grateful villagers. . . She jolted herself back to reality. But the Colonel wasn't wicked! Eccentric, perhaps and stubborn, possibly, but cast as a villain? Impossible!

Again, she lay back on the pillow, her thoughts a bewildering jumble. All that she was certain of was that Miss Ferriday, though willing, couldn't help. This meant that her letter to the Colonel was her last hope. He would have received it by now! Her eyes came to rest on the flowers he had sent her. Surely such a thoughtful man would see the sense – and the justice – in what she had written? Her gaze moved to the bird carving and the feathers and she felt tears well up and spill down her cheeks. She had to save the Peglers – and Tangleton!

Chapter 9

Perkins

It needed only a brief glance at Max's face the following morning to confirm Jenny's worst fears.

"They've gone – went last night," Max said dully, avoiding his sister's eyes. He held up a scrap of paper. "Joe left their address. I said I'd write. He's sorry he missed you."

Jenny gulped and held back the tears that stung her eyes.

"Never mind, dear," her mother said consolingly. "They'll be back, I'm sure they will. Mr Pegler's bound to find another post somewhere near. You'll see."

Jenny managed with difficulty to control her feelings as she thanked the nurses who had looked after her. Soon she found herself being helped on her crutches out of the ward, along a corridor and outside into the late summer sunshine.

"Soon have you home again, young lady!" her father said with a teasing chuckle as he helped her into the car. But Jenny failed to respond. All her hopes and plans seemed to have been reduced to nothing. The Peglers had gone, and her spirits seemed to have departed with them.

Mrs Davis asked about Miss Ferriday's letter during the

drive home and was amazed to hear that the old lady had allowed Jenny to keep the book. Mr Davis seized on the suggestion that the children should attempt to bring the local natural history up to date.

"Well, there's a challenge for you both!" he said enthusiastically. Jenny sensed that he was trying to help her forget the bad news, if only for a little while. "Should keep you both out of mischief, for a year or two at least!"

Jenny was about to tell them about the possible return of the Colonel's son, but changed her mind. After all, it wouldn't make any difference, now that the Peglers had gone. The young man's coming would probably prevent other families from being driven out, but the worst had already happened as far as she was concerned. It dawned on her at last that all her scheming to try to find some way of saving Tangleton from its fate had been nothing more than wishful thinking. In her heart she knew that she hadn't the faintest idea how to go about it. Worse still, she seemed to have lost the will to carry it out.

The holidays were almost over by now. Both Jenny and Max were feeling a little apprehensive about starting their new schools. Max had already met Miss Keynes, the headmistress of the little village school, who made no secret of her delight at welcoming a new pupil, especially as Joe and Kit Pegler had left the village.

Mr and Mrs Davis had been in touch with the headmaster of Chipping Burton Comprehensive School, and it had been arranged that Jenny would be admitted to the school on the first day of term, despite her ankle still being in plaster. She was to visit the school on the day before term started, to meet her form teacher and see the layout of the building.

The one consolation for both Jenny and Max at the departure of the Pegler children was the change in attitude of Mr Pegler himself. Obviously relieved to know that his children were no longer in danger of being taken into care, at least for the present, the keeper was now far more relaxed in his manner. This was soon apparent when he called at Oaklands a few days after Jenny arrived home.

"Glad ya like it," he replied with a shy grin when Jenny thanked him for his present of the carved woodpecker. "A pair o' them nested not far from my cabin. You could 'ear the old cock bird a-drummin' a mile off."

After adding his own thanks to the keeper, Mr Davis went on: "We've prepared a space in an outbuilding for you to store your furniture when your notice expires at the end of next month."

"And I've packed away Joe's collection," Max added, recalling with a shiver of excitement their secret night-time journey from his friend's museum down to Oaklands.

At Mr Davis's suggestion, the two men settled down to draft an advertisement for a new situation to appear in the local paper, ready for Mrs Davis to type. As there were several large estates in the neighbourhood, The Davises were hopeful that a suitable vacancy could be found.

The children's parents had also offered to accommodate Mr Pegler at Oaklands until he secured another post.

"That's very kind o' you, the keeper replied, "but I can't put you to all that trouble. I jus' can't."

"But it's no trouble – really it isn't." Mrs Davis began.

"Tell ya what," Mr Pegler interrupted. "If I end up out of a job an' with no roof over ma 'ead, I'll borrow a tent an' pitch it on your lawn 'til summat turns up!"

~~~~~~~~~

A sudden change in the weather added to the children's unsettled state. After several hot, still days, in which the sun had shone from dawn till dusk in a cloudless sky, a sombre mass of yellowish cloud built up one evening over the distant hills. A rustling breeze stealthily invaded the garden, toying with the leaves. There was an uneasy, stifling feeling in the air and Max, looking out from his bedroom window, noticed that the swallows thronging the wires along the lane, twittered agitatedly. By now the atmosphere had become sticky and intense.

"A storm's brewing – and a pretty violent one too," he heard his father say downstairs. "With luck, it'll break during the night and clear the air by tomorrow."

"I hope so," Max said to himself. "I want to make the most of what's left of the holidays."

Folding back the sheets, he climbed into bed. The heat was oppressive. He would never be able to sleep, even with all his bedclothes turned down. His thoughts turned to Joe, uprooted from the countryside he knew and loved and set down like an item of freight in the middle of a huge, unfriendly city. Poor Joe – and Kit and little George too! Although he'd never actually met them, he felt he knew them almost as well as he knew their brother. How bewildered and lost they would be, away from their father and the familiar surroundings of home. Home – Oaklands was his home now. And despite the disappointments and uncertainties, he was glad that they had left the city behind. So was Jenny. And Mum, despite the shops being so far away. And as for Dad – well, he seemed fitter and happier already. Yes, it had been a good move. . .

Drowsily, he turned on to his side. The holiday had almost gone. Tomorrow he would take his bird book and explore the area beyond the Lodge gates. He would set off early on his own journey of discovery – alone. Jenny would have to stay at home, nursing her sprained ankle. He would return triumphant, with stories of things he had seen – specimens too, perhaps . . . tomorrow . . .

He awoke with a start. A vivid flash of lightning suddenly filled the room with yellow light, followed almost immediately by a deafening crash of thunder. The house seemed to tremble and then to brace itself to withstand the next assault. Max lay motionless, awaiting the next flash, listening to the rain pounding on the roof above his head. What must it be like outside in the storm? He shuddered and nestled deeper into the bed, pulling the sheets up and over his body. Already it was cooler. The storm, it seemed, was already clearing the air.

Suddenly he stiffened. Above the hammering of the rain, his keen ear had detected another sound, faint yet unmistakable, outside. He waited, tense with concentration, to hear it again. Sure enough, after the next clap of thunder, the sound rose once more above the relentless beat of the driving rain. It was the plaintive meow of a cat!

Max groped for the torch he had kept by his bedside since the night of Joe's visit. Slipping out of bed, he glided noiselessly from his bedroom, across the landing, and down the stairs. Despite the din outside, the house itself was in silence. He pulled up abruptly at the foot of the stairs as another vivid flash illuminated the passage, revealing the familiar table with vase of flowers, pictures and prints along the wall, in a dazzling yellowish light.

He switched on the porch light and paused before the door, listening to the incessant beating of the rain against the woodwork. A puddle had formed where the wind had forced the rain through a narrow gap under the door. He hesitated. He would get soaked the moment he opened the door. Turning, he slipped on his father's waterproof that hung on a nearby peg and unfastened the lock. Opening the door a few inches, he peered outside into the darkness.

"Perkins?" he called. "Perkins – where are you?"

The rain drove into his face, stinging his skin with its impact. "Come on, Perkins!" he called again, desperately. "Don't be afraid – I won't hurt you."

Another dazzling flash of lightning tore through the blackness with a hideous jagged gash, followed almost immediately by a thunder clap directly overhead.

"Perkins! Come in – good cat!" Max pleaded, flinching in the driving rain.

Suddenly he became aware of a slight noiseless movement just beyond the pool of light thrown from the porch lamp. To his relief, a pair of greenish-yellow eyes shone out of the darkness – Perkins!

He was about to step outside towards the cat when the sleek black shape bounded in through the doorway and sat regarding him with huge enquiring eyes from inside the adjoining room. Relieved, he forced the door shut against the swirling wind.

"Perkins – you're soaked!" he whispered, shivering as he slipped out of his father's waterproof, which had already left a pool of water on the passage floor. The cat began to wash itself with sweeping flicks of its pink tongue, apparently unconcerned about its recent ordeal. Max fetched a saucer of milk and watched in silent satisfaction as the cat left off its grooming and began to lap with single-minded concentration.

"You'll be all right now, I expect," he said as Perkins turned from the empty saucer and stretched himself contentedly on the carpet. "The furniture's different from when Miss Ferriday lived here but the house is still the same."

Having satisfied himself that the cat was comfortably established in his old surroundings, Max tiptoed back upstairs to his room and snuggled back into bed. The storm, meanwhile, had begun to die away and by the time he had drifted off into sleep once more, the thunder had receded to a faint muttering many miles distant.

~~~~~~~~

Jenny was overjoyed at the appearance of Perkins. "Isn't he a beautiful cat?" she exclaimed, "And he behaves as though he's always lived here."

"He did once, remember," Mrs Davis reminded her, "before we arrived on the scene."

"I wonder why it's taken him all this time to come back?" Jenny speculated, stroking the cat's black silky fur. "Surely he could sense that he'd be welcome."

Mr Davis laughed. "It took a good old thunderstorm to drive you indoors, didn't it, Perkins?" The children laughed too as the cat, which had been purring softly under Jenny's caress, suddenly threw back its head and gave a long, gaping yawn.

Mrs Davis, however, soon cut their laughter short. "Don't get too attached to him, you two," she warned. "Remember what Miss Ferriday said in her letter."

Jenny looked up. "Oh, I know we can't keep him, if that's what you mean. We're only looking after him until he goes back to Miss Ferriday."

"But what if he won't settle at her new home?" Max asked

hopefully. "I read somewhere that cats are more faithful to homes than to owners."

"Yes – and cats have even found their way for miles back to their old home." Jenny added.

Their father nodded in agreement. "Yes, cats have a mind of their own. Old Perkins here must have sensed that that something odd was going on when Miss Ferriday started packing, and it's taken him all this time to return home."

" – which proves that Perkins wouldn't want to go and live with Miss Ferriday, doesn't it?" Max said triumphantly.

"That's up to Miss Ferriday to decide," Mrs Davis said. "He belongs to her and he obviously means a great deal to her."

Jenny buried her fingertips deeper into the rich, glossy fur. "I suppose we'll have to write to Miss Ferriday again, to ask her if she wants her cat back." she said, regret clear in her voice. "And then if she decides . . ."

"I'll write." Max interrupted.

The others turned to him in amazement. Letter-writing had always been Max's pet hate. He still owed several thank-you letters to various relatives for birthday gifts from a month earlier, which Jenny was quick to recall.

"You! You hate writing letters – and your spelling's awful!" she said scathingly. "Besides, you never wrote to thank Aunt Ann and Uncle Keith for . . ."

"That's got nothing to do with it," Max interrupted. "I'm the one who heard Perkins, remember – *and* got soaking wet persuading him to come inside. So it's only right that I should be the one to tell Miss Ferriday the good news."

"Max's right, you know, Jenny," Mrs Davis said, her hand on her daughter's shoulder.

"Of course he is," Mr Davis added, winking across at Jenny. " – and who knows? He might begin to develop the letter-writing habit and get on with all those thank-you letters he owes."

Jenny put on her give-me-strength look. "You must be joking, Dad. And anyway, Miss Ferriday will never be able to read what he writes without an interpreter."

"You'll see," Max vowed amid the ensuing laughter. "I'll write the very best letter I've ever written. You just wait and see."

Max was as good as his word. After losing count of the number of attempts, he at last completed the letter and showed it to his parents, who were quick to congratulate him on both handwriting and contents. Even Jenny admitted that he had excelled himself.

"If Miss Ferriday really does want Perkins back, Dad and I will have to take him over, somehow," said Max, carefully firming down the tab of the envelope. "And if she says we can keep him – well, that's fine, isn't it?"

His parents exchanged glances. "Yes, but don't build up too many hopes," Mr Davis warned.

Mrs Davis nodded in agreement. "We don't want you to be disappointed, that's all."

"Don't worry – we won't," Jenny replied, holding the contentedly-purring Perkins close, as though defying anyone to try to take him away.

Chapter 10

The Visitor

The last day of the summer holidays had arrived at last. Jenny, her foot still in plaster, was spending the morning at her new school, meeting her form teacher and hobbling around the huge building, trying to find her way from one department to another.

Max, meanwhile, waited impatiently for the postman's van to pull up at the gate. Both he and Jenny had written letters to Joe, posting them in one envelope at the same time as his letter to Miss Ferriday. Three days had gone by since then. Surely he would receive at least one reply today!

But no. The van chugged by Oaklands without stopping. Dejectedly, Max went back indoors and upstairs to his room. Early September sunshine streamed in through the window, mocking his low spirits. School tomorrow. A strange school, with strange children. No Joe – and no Jenny either. His sister and he had their differences but she was all right, really. Bossy at times, of course, but he knew he'd miss seeing her around at break times.

Looking absently from his bedroom window, he noticed the ample form of Perkins, sleeping contentedly beneath a clump of mallow on the border by the lawn. Lucky cat! No worries, no responsibilities – nothing to do but doze in the sunshine. Good old Perkins. He had become one of the family by now. And yet any day they could learn that Miss Ferriday wanted him back after all. So why had he been disappointed when the post van passed by? After all, it could just as easily have brought bad news as good! If only he knew! What he'd hoped for, more than anything else in the world, was that the postman would bring him a letter from Miss Ferriday, saying that they could keep Perkins. Then he could have awaited Jenny's return and told her the good news! But at least the old lady hadn't asked for her cat to be returned – yet.

He craned his neck as a car swung into the drive. Dad and Jenny were back. Mr Davis had managed to get a day's leave to drive Jenny over to see her new school. He had promised to take them both for a country drive after lunch as a last holiday treat and Max was hoping to do some bird-watching. He turned quickly from the window and hurried downstairs towards the babble of voices below.

~~~~~~~~

They returned home happily during the late afternoon, after three hours or so of leisurely sightseeing, marred only by Mrs Davis's absence. The men from the post office had promised to connect the telephone, and with no neighbours living nearby, she had stayed at home to let them in.

As the car turned the corner of the lane leading to Oaklands, Mr Davis indicated the road ahead. "We have visitors, it seems."

Jenny craned forward. "I expect it's the telephone men . . ." she began, stopping abruptly as she spotted a large black car parked near the entrance to their drive.

Max regarded her scornfully. "Whoever heard of telephone engineers in a car! Looks like a taxi to me."

Mr Davis nodded. "I think you're right, Max," he said as they drew near. "Besides, the telephone wire is already connected – look."

Sure enough, they could see a man in a dark coat was seated behind the wheel of the car. He continued to stare straight ahead as Mr Davis swung into the drive.

"I wonder who it can be?" Jenny said after her father had helped her out of the car and on to her crutches.

"We'll soon know," said Max, as they stepped indoors.

They heard the faint rattle of teacups as they paused for a moment outside the sitting-room door. Entering the room, they found their mother engaged in deep conversation with a tall, grey-haired lady, dressed in a severe dark blue costume. Her heavily-wrinkled face was of striking appearance, especially her pale blue eyes, which shone brightly as she listened to what Mrs Davis was saying. She lifted her head with interest as Jenny and Max appeared.

" – and here they are!" their mother said, turning to the children with a smile. "Children, we have a special visitor this afternoon. This lady is Miss Ferriday!"

As they stepped forward to greet their guest, Max noticed the still form of Perkins lying fast asleep in the old lady's lap. "I expect you've called to collect him," he said, trying his hardest to hide his keen sense of disappointment.

Miss Ferriday ran a deeply-veined hand through the cat's fur. "On the contrary, Max," she said with a smile. "I was so overjoyed to receive your letter, telling me of Perkins' return, that I called to ask your parents if they would be prepared to give him a home." The children's eyes sparkled with delight. "You see," Miss Ferriday continued, "Pets are frowned upon where I now live, so if, as your mother seemed to think, you are willing to keep him . . ."

"Willing?" Max gulped, scarcely able to believe his ears, "You bet we are! Aren't we, Jenny?"

"Oh yes – yes, please!" Jenny exclaimed.

"Then that's settled!" Miss Ferriday beamed. "I'm so glad." She looked down fondly at the slumbering cat. "You are a most fortunate puss, Perkins, to have such kind young people at Oaklands. I hope you appreciate that."

"I do hope that you didn't mind the children writing to you, Miss Ferriday." Mr Davis, who had been putting away the car, said after being introduced to the visitor.

"Not in the least!" Miss Ferriday exclaimed. "They have spirit, these two, and that's always good to see." She frowned. "What saddens me is that I see no possible way in which I can help them over the matter of the fate of the village. You see –"

"But you can, Miss Ferriday!" Jenny burst out. "The Colonel thinks he's pleasing you by letting the estate fall into ruin. He told us so, didn't he, Max?" Her brother nodded in agreement.

Mr and Mrs Davis exchanged looks of alarm. "You must not speak in that manner to Miss Ferriday, Jenny!" her father said severely. "We all appreciate your concern for the village and its people, but . . ."

"No – let her finish, please," Miss Ferriday interrupted, leaning forward in her chair so that the slumbering Perkins awoke and opened an enquiring eye. "Is that really what Claude – my brother – said?"

Jenny looked across doubtfully at her parents before continuing. "Yes. He said that he wanted you to know that there would be no more hunting or shooting or any other cruel sports – not even angling – on the estate."

A faraway look spread over the old lady's face. When at last she spoke, her words came slowly and quietly, as though addressed to herself. "Of course, Claude hasn't hunted for years – not since that bad fall – Lost his passion for shooting, too, I seem to recall." She paused, before giving a low chuckle. "But as for giving up his beloved rod and line – well, he certainly must have changed since I knew him. Goodness me, yes!"

"Jenny's right, Miss Ferriday!" Max blurted, amazed at his own boldness. "The Colonel said that he loves nature now in the way he used to – the way you do. You know – watching wild creatures, not killing them."

"It was the war that was to blame," Miss Ferriday continued, still in little more than a whisper. "We tend to blame the war for everything, I know, but it's true. Poor Claude. He was wounded, you know – quite badly. He came back a different man. Changed completely. Then his new friends started to arrive. Hard people, they were – out for what they could get, most of them. I hoped and prayed that Claude would see through them for what they were – but no." Her voice tailed off before resuming again in its normal lively tone. "That's how he met Eva, his wife. People said I was jealous. They accused me of trying to make trouble. They even branded me as a witch!" She gave a hollow laugh before continuing. "So I left the Hall and came to live here, at Oaklands. It seemed the only sensible thing to do. Then Eva left, too, taking their young son with her. Poor Claude. He's suffered a great deal."

Jenny, who had been following the old lady's ramblings with intense concentration, could hold back no longer. "That's why I – we – think that you should become friends again!" she said breathlessly. "I mean – Max and I quarrel – often –

but we always make it up afterwards."

Mrs Davis coughed nervously. "I think that will do for now, children."

"It certainly will!" The sternness of Mr Davis's voice made the children flinch. "Miss Ferriday has been very patient so far, listening to all you have to say. But enough's enough. It's not for you to compare –"

"But of course it's for them to compare!" Miss Ferriday interrupted him. "Shame on you, Mr Davis! It's the most natural thing in the world for them to compare. Goodness me, yes!" She looked from Max to Jenny with a warm twinkle in her eye. "We are uncomfortable with what these children say because they speak the truth. They – bless their hearts – speak their minds as a matter of course, even when it hurts. We adults talk in half-truths for most of the time, so that when we hear the plain honest truth, it offends our so-called sense of decency." The old lady had become so animated by now that Perkins, jolted from his sleep by the jerking of her body, rose to his feet in protest. Miss Ferriday gave another of her chuckles and lifted him down on to the carpet. "Do forgive me, please!" she said, smiling across at the children's parents, "I'm afraid I got carried away. It was most rude of me – I do apologise!"

The children beamed their delight. Jenny felt a sudden urge to throw her arms round the old lady's neck but with effort restrained the impulse. Mrs Davis rose to make more tea.

Seizing his opportunity, Max slipped into her chair and leaned across towards Miss Ferriday. "Do you think Mr Pegler – he's the keeper – might get his job back?" Between them, the children told their visitor about their friendship with Joe and about his unhappy exile to Manchester. Jenny went on to mention her letter to the Colonel. Miss Ferriday listened patiently, her face solemn. "Yes, my dear, your mother told me all about your rescue, and about Mr Pegler's problems," she said at last. "I agree that he deserves our help – and his little family too, poor man." She paused thoughtfully before continuing, "Of course, a gamekeeper's job is to rear pheasants and certain other birds for shooting – and to exterminate any other creatures which may prey on them. You do realise that, I hope?"

Max hesitated. "Yes. But he's a good naturalist, too . . ."

". . .and a craftsman!" Jenny added, reaching for the carving the keeper had given her. "Look, Miss Ferriday – isn't it wonderful?"

The old lady examined the carved woodpecker with admiration. "You have my promise that I will contact my brother and attempt to heal our quarrel. Claude is a reasonable man, if a little impetuous at times. Let us hope that it is not too late to reverse this unhappy decision."

"Oh, I do hope so!" Jenny declared.

"Me too. Anything to get Joe back!" added Max.

Miss Ferriday turned towards Mr Davis. "The one possible snag as I see it may be Ian's return." she said with a frown. "As I told Jenny in my letter, my nephew has recently returned from abroad and I am told that he will be coming over to Tangleton shortly."

"Need that be bad news?" Mr Davis asked.

Miss Ferriday bit her lip doubtfully. "No, not necessarily, I suppose. I have heard alarming reports of his wild behaviour, but that was years ago. We must hope that he has matured a little by now."

Soon it was time for the old lady to leave. Max carried Perkins to the gate as the entire family came outside to wave goodbye.

"I'll be in touch with my brother very soon – I promise!" Miss Ferriday called as she stepped into the car.

"Thanks for Perkins!" Max called.

"And thanks for your lovely book!" Jenny added.

"And thank you for coming, Miss Ferriday." Mrs Davis managed to get in before the driver closed the car door. "Do visit us again – soon."

"I think Miss Ferriday is the sweetest old lady I've ever met." announced Jenny as the taxi disappeared from view. "Except Grandma of course."

"And to think that people called her a witch," Max added. "Doesn't make sense."

Back inside the house, conversation turned to the Pegler family. "I vote we have a celebration party when Joe and the others come back," Max declared.

"Yes – with one of your special cakes, Mum, like you made for my birthday," Jenny added.

Mr Davis held up a warning hand. "Sorry to spoil the fun," he said, "but you mustn't bank on things happening the way we want them to. You heard what Miss Ferriday said. If the Colonel's son is anything like the tearaway he used to be, he'll want to make changes." He frowned. "And they may not be for the better."

Max looked up, puzzled. "What kind of changes, Dad?"

"I don't know," came the reply. "I only wish I did."

"Any changes would be for the better, if you ask me," Jenny

declared. "He couldn't do worse than allow Tangleton to die, could he?"

The frown remained on her father's face. "Well, let's hope not," he said.

Chapter 11

The Wanderer Returns

Max stepped out of the school gate on to the village street and headed for home. The first day hadn't been a bad as he had feared. There were only four others of his own age in the school, two boys and two girls, and they all seemed rather shy, but he had found the work interesting, even if somewhat different from what he had been used to. Miss Keynes, the headmistress, who taught all the juniors, was a tiny, bubbly woman with a deep voice and a merry laugh. She seemed to have read every children's book that had ever been written and had spent some time with him in the library corner, advising him on his choice of reading book, her oddly-pitched voice booming excitedly as she summarised the plots of the stories with great gusto.

It was not until he had bid farewell to the one boy whose homeward route lay in the same direction as his own for a short distance that Max noticed just how badly Tangleton was decaying. The once trim rows of stone-built cottages lining the village street had an unkempt, forlorn appearance, unlike anything he had ever seen. Some cottages actually lay in ruins, with spiky tufts of wiry grass emerging from the broken stonework and heaps of rubble and crumbling plaster strewn around beneath a layer of tangled weeds. Other cottages, empty and derelict, had gaping holes in their thatched roofs and rotting window frames with jagged remnants of broken glass round their edges. Even the few inhabited dwellings had peeling paintwork, odd broken window panes patched with hardboard, and gardens overgrown with neglect. How, he asked himself, could Colonel Ferriday, the quiet old man who had been so kind to Jenny, allow this to happen? He could make no sense of it at all.

He reached the end of the street at last and began the steady climb up the narrow lane towards Oaklands. Jenny was lucky. She would have completed her first day at Chipping Burton Comprehensive by now. She didn't have to face a daily walk to and from this unhappy, dying village. Thank goodness that he too would transfer there next September. He was approaching a clump of ash trees in a corner of the field alongside the lane when his watchful eye spotted a flicker of small wings in the topmost branches. What were the birds? Chaffinches, perhaps, or maybe tits of some kind? He stopped and looking upwards, searched the swaying treetops.

Just then, the roar of a car engine made him swing round in alarm. There was a screech of brakes as a sleek, high-powered sports car hurtled round the bend towards him and thundered by in a cloud of dust, its horn blaring, causing him to throw himself into the nearby hedge for safety. Startled and angry, Max scrambled back on to the lane, shaking his fist after the departing car, which could still be heard continuing its noisy and reckless way up the hill beyond Oaklands to – its destination could be one place, and one place only – Tangleton Hall. And its driver could be only one person – Ian, Colonel Ferriday's son.

Mrs Davis listened to Max's account of his encounter with the sports car with tight lips. "You might have been killed, Max!" she said after she had heard the full story. "From what you say, it seems that Miss Ferriday's worse fears have come true."

"I just hope that Ian soon gets bored with life at the Hall and goes back to – to wherever he came from," Max said with feeling. "By the way, is there a letter for me, Mum?"

His mother shook her head. "Afraid not, Max. There's one for Jenny, with the local postmark, that's all."

Max looked glum. "I had hoped to get a letter from Joe," he said sadly. Just then, they heard the sound of a car pulling into the drive and Jenny hobbled in, her face glowing. "It's great, Mum! My form teacher takes us for art, too. You should see her drawings – super!"

As Mrs Davis, with Max's help, related to her husband the incident with the sports car, Jenny eagerly opened her letter. "It's from Colonel Ferriday!" she announced excitedly. "Listen, everybody!"

Tangleton Hall,

Tangleton

4th September

My Dear Jenny,

By the time you receive this letter, you will be out of hospital. I do so hope that your recovery is both rapid and complete, and that you like your new school and soon make many new friends, which I am sure you will.

Concerning the other matter, I must confess that you put me in something of a spot! Of what use is a gamekeeper when one ceases to rear game? As you know, I am allowing the park to return to the wild, and the game must take their chance, along with all the other creatures! Nev-

ertheless, your plea on Pegler's behalf is so eloquent and direct that I find it hard to ignore.

This is what I propose to do. Ian, my son, is due to return very shortly *and may make his home here. I will consult with him about Pegler's future. He may well have some ideas on the subject. Anyway, rest content that somehow, some way will be found to resolve Pegler's present unhappy situation, either by finding him employment of some kind on the estate, or perhaps by assisting him to obtain a keeper's post with some other employer.*

I do hope that this will set your mind at rest, young lady.

Yours very truly,

Claude Ferriday.

Jenny looked from one parent to the other triumphantly. "Well, that's nice of him, isn't it?" she said. "After all, it's a promise that Joe's family won't just be thrown out at the end of the month. And then when Miss Ferriday patches up their quarrel, perhaps . . ."

"What exactly did you put in that letter, Jenny?" Mr Davis demanded, in a tone that caused his daughter's voice to trail away in mid-sentence. His face had lost none of its grimness since hearing about Max's encounter with the sports car.

"I – I asked Colonel Ferriday to give Mr Pegler his job back – that's all," Jenny faltered, taken aback by her father's sternness.

"All?" Mr Davis repeated, his voice rising. "Don't you realise, Jenny, what a serious matter this is? Not content with offering your advice to Miss Ferriday when she called, you write along similar lines to the Colonel, without either Mum's or my knowledge."

Jenny was about to try to justify her actions but instead turned appealingly to her mother.

"I'm sorry, Jenny, but Dad's right," Mrs Davis said, quietly but firmly. "We share your concern for the Peglers – and for the village, too – but you really must learn to think before you take the law into your own hands. We hadn't the heart to reprimand you after your fall in the quarry but by acting as you did, you could have got yourself killed . . ."

". . . and Mr Pegler and Joe saved me!" Jenny burst out. "So I had to help them too. Don't you see?" Mr and Mrs Davis exchanged glances. Jenny, sobbing bitterly by now, sought comfort in her mother's arms. Mr Davis waited patiently for his daughter to recover a little before continuing in quieter tones, "You did what you thought best, Jenny. Mum and I accept that and are proud of you because of it. But don't forget that we too have the Peglers' interests at heart. We offered Mr Pegler and the children a temporary home here, don't forget. We are storing their furniture. I am helping Mr Pegler to find another post and Mum is going to help him to read and write."

Max looked up, puzzled. "But you're not a teacher, Mum,"

His mother smiled. "No, Max, that's true," she replied. "But I did take a course on adult literacy a few years ago and I should find out whether it's of any use tonight."

"Tonight – why tonight?" Max asked.

"Because Mr Pegler is coming down for his first lesson tonight – very soon, in fact," Mr Davis said, "so let's all calm down, shall we, and forgive and forget?" He put his arm round Jenny. "I'm sorry, love, honest I am. And I really do congratulate you on getting the Colonel to agree to help Mr Pegler.

That was some achievement!"

"It certainly was!" Mrs Davis added. "Who knows – perhaps he's seen Mr Pegler already, now that his son's arrived. He may have good news for us when he comes down."

Max, however, could not forget the incident with the sports car. "I just hope the Colonel's son treats Mr Pegler better than he treated me," he said glumly.

Jenny, who had been trying hard to regain her composure, allowed her eyes to meet her father's for the first time since his stern words. "Let's hope that the Colonel puts him in his place," she said. "It's a father's job, after all."

They sat up expectedly as the bell rang. "Let Mr Pegler talk to Mum and me alone first," Mr Davis said. "He may feel a little embarrassed to begin with if we're all around. You'll hear everything eventually, don't worry."

Jenny nodded. "I've got some homework to do, anyway, What about you, Max?"

"I'll come as well," came the answer. "You will be sure to ask about Joe, won't you?" he reminded his parents.

His mother smiled and tousled his hair. "You can ask him yourself later if you like, before he leaves," she said.

Both children found concentration difficult. They could hear the faint murmur of conversation from downstairs and further distraction was provided by Perkins, who could not decide which of the children's rooms appealed to him most, and had to be let in and out at regular intervals. Max, who was dividing the pages of his bird-spotter's notebook into headed columns, sudden stiffened attentively. The roar of a car engine, faint at first, now shattered the calm outside, as it hurtled down the hill past the house towards the village.

"That was Ian Ferriday," he called to his sister.

Jenny sat with her pencil poised above her book. "Maybe he's going. Could be the Colonel's sent him packing," she called back hopefully.

Max returned to his task. "Umm. Sounds too good to be true," he replied.

A few minutes later, Jenny's door opened and her father entered. Jenny looked up. "We just heard the sports car go past, Dad. Do you think the Colonel's son has gone?"

"I doubt it. Off for a night's drinking, more likely," Mr Davis replied, his face grim.

Max followed his father into the room. "What's wrong, Dad?" he asked anxiously.

Jenny, too, sensed trouble. "Is it something to do with Mr Pegler, Dad?" she demanded.

Their father propped himself awkwardly on the edge of a chair. "Bad news, I'm afraid," he said with downcast eyes. "Mr Pegler won't be staying on, after all."

Max broke the stunned silence that followed. "But – but why not?" he protested. "The Colonel more or less promised. He said . . ."

"I know full well what he said, Max," Mr Davis interrupted wearily. "You might as well know the entire truth. There was a meeting between the Colonel, his son, and Mr Pegler a short time ago. The Colonel said that he wanted Mr Pegler to stay after all but Ian, his son, disagreed. He said that Mr Pegler had not done his job properly – not controlled the vermin. He even accused him of shooting pheasants and selling them."

"That's a lie – a wicked lie. I know it is!" Jenny blazed angrily.

"Of course it is!" added Max, equally outraged. "Surely the Colonel didn't believe him!"

Their father sighed unhappily. "I don't suppose he did, but the damage had been done," he said. "Mr Pegler denied the charges of course, and demanded that young Ferriday withdraw them. He refused. There was a terrible row and Mr Pegler walked out. He's very upset. He says that he wouldn't stay and work for Ian Ferriday, even if he offered to double his pay – and I don't blame him."

Max's bottom lip quivered. "The Colonel must be a coward, otherwise he'd have thrown Ian out – I would!" he announced, close to tears.

"I can understand you feeling like that, Max," his father said. "But remember that Ian is the Colonel's only son. He hasn't seen him for years. I expect he'll take a firmer line with him when he finds out what an unpleasant character he is."

Jenny, too, was struggling to hold back the tears. "He should be able to see that already – everyone else can," she said bitterly.

"Did Mr Pegler say how Joe was?" Max asked in a dull whisper.

Mr Davis produced a crumpled scrap of paper. "Yes, he's well. He sent you this note. It came with a letter to his father from their relatives in Manchester."

"Thank Mr Pegler for bringing it, please," Max said. "I think I'll go to bed now. Read it in my room. Goodnight."

Jenny dabbed her eyes. "I'm off to bed, too," she said.

Their father nodded. "I'll tell Mr Pegler that you've both gone to bed early. Had a hard first day at school. He'll understand."

Jenny began to collect her books and put them in her school bag. "Yes, say that, please," she said, "Goodnight, Dad."

~~~~~~~~

"Goodnight then, Mr Pegler."

"G'night. An' thank your wife again for a grand supper, please – an' for th' readin'."

"Don't mention it. Wish we could help more. Are you sure you won't take a room here? Space is no problem, as I said before."

"Thanks all th' same – but no. Mind you, if I see much o' th' Colonel's son, I'll not stay to work th' month out!"

"Let's hope not then. Goodnight."

"G' night, Mr Davis."

Max waited until the keeper's footsteps faded into the distance before slipping out of bed and along the landing. He tapped lightly on Jenny's door. "Are you asleep, Jen?"

"No," came the subdued reply from within.

"May I come in?"

A pause. "I suppose so – if you must."

Max tiptoed inside, closing the door quietly behind him. "Mr Pegler's just gone."

"I know. I heard the gate click."

"I've brought Joe's letter. Thought you might like to read it."

"Thanks." Jenny screwed up her eyes in an effort to decipher the sprawling script, written with a blunt pencil. "He's at school."

"I know. Started last week – before us."

"Probably better for him, anyway. And for Kit. Keep them occupied – out of trouble."

"Let's hope so." Max hesitated for a moment. "What's going to happen, Jen?"

"Happen?"

"About Mr Pegler – and the village – and, – well – everything."

"How should I know?"

Max tried again. "Well, you're the one for ideas. Don't say you haven't got any."

Jenny frowned. "I'm not risking anything just yet, not after what Dad said before dinner."

Max nodded slowly. "Yes, I know what you mean. But what do you hope will happen?"

Jenny thought for a while before replying. "I hope – " she paused, framing her thoughts. "I hope that Miss Ferriday will be able to get the Colonel to see sense and send that awful Ian packing, but . . ."

"But what?"

"I've just remembered something that Grandma used to say about problems sometimes solving themselves without us having to do anything about them. I can't remember the exact words though."

"Let's hope that it turns out like that, then. Lots of Grandma's sayings do."

"Yes. Goodnight."

"Goodnight, Jen."

Chapter 12

The Dream

The rest of the week passed uneventfully. Homework occupied most of Jenny's time during the evenings. Max, meanwhile, spent a good deal of his spare time mounting a set of bird-identification charts on his bedroom wall. Mrs Davis had been vaguely aware of an increase in the amount of traffic passing Oaklands during the week. She mentioned this to Mr Pegler when he called for his next reading lesson on Thursday evening.

The keeper frowned. "It's goin' ta be a wild weekend, if ya ask me."

"Wild?" Mr Davis enquired.

Mr Pegler nodded. "Shootin' all day an' celebratin' all night – or so I'm told."

"But I thought that the Colonel had forbidden shooting and that – " Mrs Davis began.

Mr Pegler grunted. "An' so 'e did, but Mister 'igh an' Mighty's in charge now, or so it seems, any'ow."

"And the celebrations?" Mr Davis asked, puzzled.

The keeper snorted in contempt. "Return o' the prodigal

son, I suppose – an' all 'is 'angers-on wi' 'im. I've spent all week rakin' around for beaters. There'll be more guns than pheasants from what I've bin told."

Mrs Davis shuddered. "Thank goodness we're no closer to the Hall. The extra traffic is bad enough."

"Ya might get some free entertainment if th' wind's in th' right direction," Mr Pegler said with a wry grin. "They're 'avin' dancin' on th' terrace, an' a pop group, an' 'eaven knows what else."

Max and Jenny, who had been listening to the conversation with growing alarm, exchanged glances of dismay. "But what will Colonel Ferriday do?" Jenny asked.

Mr Pegler shrugged. "Spend th' weekend in 'is wine cellar, wi' 'is ears stuffed up wi' cotton wool, if 'e's got any sense," he said drily.

By Saturday morning, the lane past Oaklands was alive with activity. Tradesmen's vans and cars packed with people moved by in a steady stream and there was much screeching of brakes and impatient blasting of horns as vehicles travelling in opposite directions met one another midway between passing places on the narrow twisting lane. Surveying the scene from Jenny's bedroom window, the children saw a straggling band of men and youths, equipped with sticks, threading their way up the lane, pausing at intervals to rest for a chat or to allow traffic to pass.

"Beaters," Max commented grimly. "John Blockley at school said his brother was taking part. They have to hit the bushes with their sticks to make the pheasants fly so that the men with guns can shoot them." He gave a sudden laugh. "Mr Pegler told John's brother to wear something bright so that the shooters would see him. He said that some of Ian's friends didn't know one end of a gun from the other."

Jenny spun round indignantly. "I don't see anything funny about that – and I'm surprised that you do!" she snapped. "You're supposed to be a bird watcher, yet you joke about all those birds being killed – ugh!"

"It was the way he said it that was funny," Max replied uncomfortably. "Of course I hate birds being shot – even pheasants. But rearing pheasants for shooting is Mr Pegler's job. It's part of country life and we've got to accept it, even if we don't agree with it, like Dad said."

"I don't want to argue," said Jenny, turning away. 'I want to get on with my geography, if you don't mind."

"I was going, anyway," Max replied, taking the hint. "Dad wants some help in the garden."

Mr Davis had started clearing an area of the garden that had clearly been untouched for years. As Max, approached, he could see his father attacking a jungle of sprawling weeds, while nearby a wisp of white smoke from a bonfire rose between the branches of a gnarled old apple tree, its earthy tang filling the air and tickling the nostrils.

Max picked up a rake and began heaping the newly-up-rooted weeds alongside the fire. Father and son worked together in silence for some time. Mellow September sunshine filtered through the apple boughs, lending a warm glow to the small, scabby fruit dotted about in the leafy branches. Max stretched up and picked one of the few apples within his reach, examining its rough yellow peel critically before taking a tentative bite.

His father looked up enquiringly. "Well – any good?"

Max grimaced. "Not too bad. A bit woody, but edible –

just!"

Mr Davis rested on his spade. "Yes, the old tree ought to come up, really. It's had its day. Besides, it's taking all the light. There's room for three or four young trees there." He stiffened. "Hear that? The shoot's started."

The crack of gunfire echoed from the direction of the woods. Suddenly Max recalled with a shudder the memory of Jenny's fall down the quarry and his frantic search for Mr Pegler's cabin. "Shall we cut it down now, Dad?"

"Now?" his father replied in surprise. "Well, we could do, I suppose. The cutting-down part should be easy enough. It'll be the grubbing up of the roots that will be the test."

"It'll take our minds off the shooting," Max continued. "– and provide logs for winter."

"Right then," his father said. "There's no time like the present – come on."

"And we should never put off until tomorrow what can be done today, as Grandma never tires of saying," added Max.

As Mr Davis had predicted, felling the old tree proved fairly straightforward. They were joined eventually by Mrs Davis and Jenny. Mrs Davis helped Max to carry branches to the bonfire while Jenny hobbled around collecting the best of the apples to make into apple chutney, a great favourite with the family. Max and his father, meanwhile, struggled with pick and spade to sever the thick, sinewy roots at the base of the stump. They could hear the sound of gunfire throughout the afternoon but no one commented on the slaughter taking place in the nearby woods.

Jenny was soon tired by the activity and returned to her room to finish her homework. As teatime approached, Mrs

Davis, too, went back indoors to prepare the meal.

"We're almost there!" Mr Davis gasped, mopping the sweat from his brow. He passed Max the pick and climbed out of the hole they had excavated. "Here, yours can be the honour of severing the last root while I attend to the fire."

Wearily, Max swung the pick. At least, the hard work had taken his mind off all that was going on in the woods. One final blow and the root snapped, causing the stump to slew over to one side. "Timber!" he shouted in triumph, withdrawing the pick from the tangle of severed roots. Just then, something caught his eye. He bent down to see closer. Yes, a shiny green object – glass. With mounting curiosity he scraped away the soil. Whatever it was, the object had been wedged under the main root and had somehow escaped being struck by his pick. At last, his fingers closed around it and raised it into view – a bottle. But what a bottle! Max gazed in wonder at his find. Made of thick, dark green glass, the bottle had a tapering neck, pinched near the top to hold a small green marble. The sides were embossed with an ornate design and the name and address of the brewery company.

"Dad!" Max called excitedly. "Look what I've found!"

~~~~~~~~~

Max, sitting with a bird magazine, yawned. The fresh air and hard work had left him with a pleasant, glowing tiredness. Despite the shooting, he'd enjoyed the day. And finding the old bottle had put the seal of perfection on it. After wiping off most of the dirt, he had put it safely in the garage. He'd take Dad's advice and not wash it for a day or two, allowing it to be exposed to the air. Then he intended showing it to his mother and sister. His first old bottle find – and what a beauty! One day, when Joe returned, he'd show it to him. He'd be impressed too! Those eyes behind the thick glasses would open wider than ever as he listened to the story of how the bottle came to light. Good old Joe. When he came back to Tangleton at last they'd go off on bird-watching expeditions and dig up fantastic old bottles and . . .

"Max!"

He woke and sat up with a start to find the smiling face of his father looking down at him.

"You dropped off to sleep, old fellow!" Mr Davis said. "I just slipped out to bank up the bonfire for the night and when I got back, I found you in the land of Nod!"

Max rubbed his eyes and stretched. "Where's Mum?"

"In the other room, watching television. Jenny's getting ready for bed. It's late, you know."

Max got to his feet. "That's where I'm off. Goodnight, Dad."

"Goodnight, son," his father said. "– and thanks for all your help in the garden. I hope that the revelry doesn't keep you awake."

"It won't," Max replied, stifling a yawn.

~~~~~~~~

He hovered somewhere midway between sleep and consciousness. Perhaps, if he tried, he could continue the adventure which seemed to have come to an abrupt end. Relax, that was the secret, he told himself. Just relax and allow himself to float back into that dream world he had been so reluctant to leave – a warm, glowing place in which he was surrounded by people he knew, familiar faces, actors all in a strange story in which he was both participant and spectator.

It had begun with Miss Ferriday. She had been a witch, but a good witch. He had knocked at the door of her home, Oaklands, and she had asked him in. He had known no fear. Perkins, her cat, had jumped up on to his knee and promptly fallen asleep. The room had been filled with an intense golden light. Miss Ferriday had held a strange-looking bottle before his eyes and invited him to look into it. He had been enchanted by what it revealed.

He had seen himself entering a forest of huge towering trees, all bathed in the same golden glow. And then he had noticed the birds – strange, pheasant-like birds with plumage of breathtaking beauty – strutting through the woodland glades, everywhere he looked. Suddenly, from a hut under the trees, had emerged Mr Pegler and Joe, as though to welcome him. Then Jenny, too, had arrived on the scene and together the three children had run lightly and effortlessly through the forest, towards an even more dazzling glow, which spread across the horizon and seemed to cover the trees with molten gold. On and on they ran, until suddenly a splendid palace had loomed into view, etched in gold. On the steps had stood Colonel Ferriday, his arms outstretched in welcome –

But no, try as he would, the dream-story would not continue. Even the image of the Colonel, beckoning from the steps, began to fade. The real world, the outside world, was claiming him back, closing the magic portal, transporting him, reluctantly, to wakefulness. And yet, something remained. Far from losing its power like the rest of the dream, the golden glow showed no sign of diminishing. In fact, its strength was such that it began to hurt his eyes, pricking them, forcing them open.

It was then that he became aware of the smell. Burning! Something was burning! Dad's bonfire – out of control! The blaze spreading – to the garage – the house! He leapt out of bed and groped his way to the window. Light – a vivid yellow light – filled the room. He tore back the curtains and looked out. The sight that met his eyes made him step back aghast. The entire northern horizon was engulfed in dazzling light! The glow was at its most intense on the crest of the hill, where the drive to the Hall plunged between the trees. Pungent smoke carried on the night breeze irritated his nostrils. Tiny fragments of soot, wafted in through the open window, were settling on his face and hands. This was no bonfire!

He turned from the window in panic. "Dad! Mum!" he cried, rushing out of his room and along the landing. "Wake up quickly! There's a fire! I think it's the Hall!"

Chapter 13

Fire!

Alone in his cabin in the woods, Mr Pegler looked up from the reading exercise Mrs Davis had given him. As though this wasn't difficult enough, the din from the Hall terrace made concentration impossible. He half-wished that he'd stayed at Keeper's Cottage until the end of the month. At least the noise wouldn't have been quite so bad. But the idea of living there on his own, even if only for a few weeks, without the children, was unthinkable – the place held too many memories. It would have been too much to bear.

Wearily, he pushed the book to one side and picked up his woodcarving, a half-finished badger. He was hoping to complete it before he left Tangleton. Might be able to sell it in one of the antique-type shops in Chipping Burton. After all, the Davis's seemed quite impressed by the woodpecker he'd given Jenny. Certainly, the money would come in handy – he'd need to send some to Doreen in Manchester pretty soon. Couldn't expect her to keep the kids for nothing. The kids! He realised with a pang how much he missed them. The heart seemed to have gone out of him since they'd left. He'd lost interest in everything. Couldn't be bothered even to cook himself a meal, as his rumbling stomach was quick to remind him.

If only he could be sure that he would get another job. The old Colonel had said that he would do his best to fix him up on one of the neighbouring estates, but he'd lost touch with the other landowners years ago. And his son wouldn't lift a finger to help, of that he was certain. Not that he would accept help from such a man, anyway – he'd starve rather! At least, the Davis's were doing all they could for him, though why, he couldn't think. They owed him nothing, nothing at all. Nice folks – and a couple of grand kids, too. Though why on earth they should choose to come and live in a run-down hole like Tangleton, he couldn't for the life of him understand.

As he worked at the carving, he went over the day's events in his mind. He'd hated the shooting – always had. Watching animals and birds, not killing them, was his passion, and had been for as long as he could remember. He was still at his happiest lying motionless behind a log, watching young fox cubs at play or climbing to a hole in a tree to feel the warm round eggs in an owl's nest. There had been a time when he had dared to hope he'd find a job that involved caring for wild creatures. Instead, he had ended up rearing game birds for rich folks to slaughter! And now, here he was, widowed and with three kids to support, and soon to be out of a job altogether!

His lips formed a slow smile of grim satisfaction. At least he'd provided plenty of pheasants for the guns today. That was one in the eye for Mr High and Mighty Ian Ferriday! So much for his lies and accusations! Pompous ass! Heaven help Tangleton if he really had returned to stay. Not that he'd be here to see it, anyway.

He paused from his carving and rubbed his hand across his brow. His eyes were beginning to feel sore and tired with concentrating on the delicate work by the light of the oil lamp. He'd better call it a day and turn in, otherwise he'd let the knife blade slip and spoil the carving. Whether he'd be able to sleep with that thumping row going on over at the Hall was another matter.

~~~~~~~~~

He awoke with a start to find the cabin bathed in vivid yellowy-orange light, and the tang of smoke thick in the air. What the devil! He jumped from his rough low bunk and rushed to the cabin door. The crackle of flames confirmed his worst fears – the Hall was ablaze! Without further thought, he pulled on his clothes, stuck his feet into his wellingtons, and grabbed the axe he had used when rescuing Jenny from the quarry. Soon, he was charging through the woods towards the fire. Fools – idiotic fools, every one of them!

A scene of utter confusion confronted him as he burst through the trees and on to the Hall drive. Young men and women, clad in an assortment of strange clothes, were rushing about in blind panic, shouting and screaming hysterically above the roar of the flames, which leapt hungrily from several windows of the upper storey of the great building.

He recognised the figure of Ian Ferriday looming out of the smoke-filled air, flailing his arms wildly and shouting unintelligible commands which no-one seemed to be heeding.

"Is everybody out?" Mr Pegler demanded.

"What?" The young man spun round, his eyes wild with terror. "Oh, it's you, Pegler. Er – yes. That is – I think so. I – we – were all on the terrace when it started. Someone must have left a lighted cigarette in one of the bedrooms. I was just – "

"What about th' Colonel an' 'is staff?" the keeper interrupted.

"Oh!" The young man's jaw sagged open. "We – I – gave Hicks the evening off. I – I – don't know about Father and the Bannister woman." He dithered indecisively, and started rubbing at a sooty smear on his jacket. "But the fire brigade's on its way, Pegler. They'll soon have things under control. In the meantime I suggest you make yourself useful by – "

"Out o' my way, ya block'ead!" Mr Pegler thundered. "Folks' lives are at risk, don't ya realise that? Ev'ry second counts. I'm goin' in!" He swept past the protesting figure and made for the nearest door. Once inside, he paused for a moment to get his bearings. Yes, Mrs Bannister's room was the nearest, somewhere above. This was the wing in which the fire was raging at its fiercest. The Colonel's room in the far wing should be safe – for the present, at least. Grimly, he made for the stairs. A cloud of suffocating smoke met him as he reached the landing. He grabbed a towel from an empty room, wet it in a wash basin, and wrapped it round his face before pressing on.

Mrs Bannister lay unconscious outside her room. Staggering under her weight, the keeper struggled down the smoke-filled stairs, swinging his axe to smash through any obstructions blocking his path. He must hurry. Still the Colonel to rescue yet! To his relief, his groping hand at last located a door on to the terrace. Choking, he collapsed with his burden into the outside air as the wail of approaching fire engines broke upon his ears.

~~~~~~~~

"Not you again, Jenny?" the duty nurse looked up with a welcoming smile. "It's barely a week since we discharged you! What is it this time?"

The Davis's laughed. "She's not here as a patient this time, thank goodness!" Mr Davis explained. "She's a mere visitor now, like the rest of us."

The nurse rose from her desk. "Oh, of course!" she replied. "It's Mr Pegler you've come to see. I'll show you the way," adding over her shoulder "He's recovering remarkably well."

"And I've brought some flowers for Mrs Bannister, too," said Jenny. "I'll take them to her later, if I may."

They found the keeper sitting up in bed, Mrs Davis's reading book propped up before him. He looked up with a self-conscious grin as they entered the ward. Jenny was quick to notice two other get-well cards on the bedside table in addition to the one they had sent.

"We have a special rule for a special patient, don't we, Mr Pegler?" the nurse sang out cheerily, advancing towards the bed. "Heroes are allowed four visitors, instead of two!"

Greetings over, the Davis family settled down round the bed. They were amazed to find their friend in such good shape, considering his recent ordeal.

"I like your cards, Mr Pegler," Jenny said admiringly.

"Aye. That one's from Joe an' Kit an' George," the keeper said proudly, indicating the nearest card. "Bet ya can't guess who t'other's from, though," he added with a chuckle.

"Look and see," he went on, "Go on!"

Jenny picked up the card, an expensive one with a distinctive design.

"Well, lass, what are ya waitin' for? Read out aloud what it says," came the order. "Nurse read it ta me this mornin' but I

122

can't recall th' exact words."

Jenny opened the card and immediately recognised Colonel Ferriday's neatly-formed handwriting. She cleared her throat, surprised to find herself feeling a little nervous. "Thank God you're safe. Best wishes for a speedy recovery. Will be in contact regarding your future as soon as you leave hospital. Sincerely yours, Claude Ferriday."

"Nice o' 'im writin' wasn't it?" Mr Pegler said. "Can't think what 'e wants ta see me 'bout, though, can you?"

Mr and Mrs Davis looked at one another. "Well, I'm sure he wants to thank you properly, to begin with." Mr Davis said. "After all, you did save his housekeeper's life. And you'd have tried to rescue him, too, if the fire brigade hadn't arrived when it did."

"Somebody 'ad ta do summat," the keeper said, "Them young folks were millin' around gettin' nowhere – that prize nitwit Mr 'igh an' Mighty 'specially."

"We've seen the last of him, thank goodness!" Mrs Davis said. "Apparently the Colonel told him never to set foot on the estate again."

Mr Davis nodded. "– not that he'd have stayed, anyway, after what happened."

"Glad ta 'ear that," Mr Pegler said, "Even so, I can't see what all th' fuss is about."

Responding to a furtive nudge from his wife, Mr Davis came to the point that the Davis's had intended making all along. "Oh, before I forget, Mr Pegler, we have a room ready at Oaklands for when they discharge you from here and – " he continued, ignoring the keeper's attempt to interrupt "– this time, we won't accept 'no' for an answer!"

~~~~~~~~

Colonel Ferriday kept his word. The day after Mr Pegler left hospital, Mr Hicks called at Oaklands with the message that the Colonel, who was staying for the time being at the White Hart at Chipping Burton, wished to meet Mr Pegler there as soon as possible. Mr Davis, too, was invited to attend.

The keeper, who was absorbed in helping Max with a drawing of a sparrowhawk, squirmed uncomfortably on hearing the news. "I don't fancy goin' there – posh place like that," he said. "If th' Colonel wants ta talk business, what's wrong wi' my cabin? Or th' Rose an' Crown at Tangleton, come ta that."

Mr and Mrs Davis held a hurried consultation and it was agreed that Colonel Ferriday should be invited over to Oaklands for the meeting, the excuse being given that Mr Pegler had not fully recovered from his ordeal.

Later that evening the telephone rang. It was the Colonel. He accepted the invitation and asked whether it would be in order to bring along a friend, who had an interest in the matter to be discussed. This was agreed and the meeting was fixed for the following evening.

~~~~~~~~

Jenny looked up from her book as the drone of a car engine, followed by the crunch of tyres on the gravel below, announced the arrival of the expected visitors. "They're here, Max!", she called, hobbling over to the window. Max joined her and together they craned their necks in an effort to see who was getting out of the car. However, the overhanging front porch blocked their view and all they could see was the top of Mr Hicks's head as he opened and closed the car doors.

"I wonder who the Colonel's friend is," Max said, turning away disappointed.

"Dad said it'll most likely be another landowner," Jenny replied. "Let's hope that whoever he is, he's got a good job to offer Mr Pegler."

"And let's hope as well that it's somewhere not too far away, so that we can still see plenty of Joe." Max added as he crossed the landing back to his own room.

Half an hour or so passed and then the children heard a door below open.

"Jenny, Max!" their father called. "Will you both come down and into the drawing room, please?"

The children hurried out of their rooms and met at the top of the stairs.

"What do you suppose . . .?" Max began.

"Come on. We'll soon find out," his sister replied, grabbing his arm.

Five pairs of eyes looked up in warm greeting as they entered the room. Seated on either side were their parents. Next to Mr Davis, his bearded face beaming, sat Mr Pegler. And there, in the centre of the little group, sharing the couch, sat the Colonel and Miss Ferriday.

Chapter 14

Celebration

The children stood in the centre of the group, their eyes moving from one smiling face to the next, in utter blissful bewilderment. The Colonel was the first to speak.

"Welcome, my dear young people – welcome!" he said, in a voice thick with emotion.

"This is the highlight of our meeting. This sets the seal on a happy, happy occasion. Do join us!"

"Well, make room for them then, Claude!" Miss Ferriday said, laughing her tinkling laugh and giving him a gentle push, at the same time moving away from her brother. "Squeeze in here, both of you."

Satisfied that Jenny and Max were comfortably seated, the Colonel went on: "We thought it best to spare you the full details of our discussion, in case you found them tedious. They are now successfully concluded, I'm glad to say, so it only remains for me to . . ."

Miss Ferriday let out another merry peal of laughter, almost losing her balance in her mirth so that Max reached out in alarm to steady her. Meanwhile Perkins, who had been asleep on her lap, looked up ruefully and picked his way across to

Jenny.

"Really, Claude!" the old lady cried, "You're not addressing a board meeting! You're telling these two splendid children the wonderful news – or supposed to be!"

For a moment, the Colonel looked somewhat taken aback but his face soon creased into his former smile. "Oh, very well, Rachel, you're the talker – always were. You can explain." He gave Max a knowing wink.

Miss Ferriday cleared her throat. "Children, thanks to you, my dear brother and I are happily reunited." She looked intently at Jenny. "Our silly quarrel is over and done with and we are planning to make a fresh start." The Colonel nudged Jenny lightly with his elbow, nodding approvingly. "As you know," Miss Ferriday went on, "the Hall was badly damaged by the fire. It may have to be demolished – we're not sure yet. In any case, it's far too big for our needs so we have decided to have the Lodge restored and to live there." She paused for a moment, before fixing her gaze on Mr Pegler. "And now we come to the part that our friend Mr Pegler will play in our plans." Her gaze moved first to Max and then to Jenny. "We have decided that the park and woods shall be designated as a nature reserve." Max's eyes shone with delight. "Mr Pegler will be appointed as warden of the reserve," Miss Ferriday went on, "and Keeper's Cottage will be completely modernised, ready for his family . . ."

". . .and re-named Warden's Cottage!" Mr Pegler interrupted triumphantly.

"Now it's my turn again!" the Colonel said with a chuckle. "We shall need a team of maintenance workers for the nature reserve. It will of course be by far the largest in the county."

"Super!" Max gulped.

"The unoccupied cottages in the village will be repaired to provide homes for these people," Colonel Ferriday continued, "and steps will be taken to ensure that Tangleton once more becomes the thriving, happy place that it was in former times." He looked from Max to Jenny. "How does that sound to you both, eh?"

"Wonderful!" Jenny exclaimed, rubbing her hands together in delight. "– absolutely wonderful!"

~~~~~~~~

Accommodation at Oaklands was stretched to capacity for the few weeks prior to the Peglers moving back up the hill and into their renovated cottage. Max, who had given up his room for the Pegler children, had to make do with a sleeping bag on the floor of Jenny's room. His sister had developed the annoying habit of starting a conversation just as he was on the point of dropping off to sleep and tonight was no exception.

"Max – are you still awake?"

"Yes. What is it?"

"I've been thinking."

"Uh?"

"You remember the day when we first met Joe?"

"Uh uh."

"He called this the witch's house. Remember?"

"He meant Miss Ferriday."

"I know, stupid!"

"Well, she's not a witch."

"I know that too, but . . ."

"But what?"

"Well, he said that folks in the village believed that Miss Ferriday had cast a spell on the Colonel – her brother so that he'd never smile again."

"Just a rumour. Rubbish."

"Yes, I know, but . . ."

"Shut up, Jen and go to sleep. I'm tired."

"I will in a minute. Just let me tell you this."

"Must you?"

"Yes. Listen. Joe never got round to finishing it."

"Finishing what?"

"The spell."

"He didn't?"

"No. So I asked him tonight to finish it, and he did."

"Well?"

"Well what?"

"The spell. How did it finish?"

"The Colonel would never smile again – until his son returned."

"Well, he has, or at least, he did. And made a right mess of things, too."

"I know."

"Besides, the Colonel's happy enough now, isn't he? Goes to show that the spell business was rubbish all along – like I said."

"I know. But . . ."

"Oh no, not again – please!"

"Look, just supposing that the spell had been real . . ."

". . . which it wasn't."

"I know that. But just supposing it had been."

"Well – what then?"

"Well, the Colonel *didn't* smile again until his son came back, really, did he?"

"I don't follow."

"Look. If that horrid Ian hadn't come back, and the Hall hadn't been burnt down, Miss Ferriday and the Colonel wouldn't have patched up their quarrel. And so the Colonel wouldn't have smiled again."

"Oh, I see what you're getting at – I think. But *we* helped to bring them together, don't forget. The Colonel said so himself."

"Yes, I know we did. But it's fun trying to puzzle out why things happen as they do."

"It's not my idea of fun. Not at this time of night, anyway."

"Sorry I've kept you awake. I agree with you, of course. Spells are just rubbish."

"Of course. Like I said to begin with."

"Yes, okay. Goodnight, Max."

"Goodnight, Jen."

~~~~~~~~~

The official opening ceremony of the Tangleton Park Nature Reserve took place one pleasant April afternoon in the following spring. Television cameras, newspaper reporters and dignitaries of every kind were all present for the occasion. Almost everyone from Tangleton village was there, too. The old people, who said it was the most memorable event they could recall, were ferried up to the Park in a convoy of cars, specially arranged by Colonel Ferriday.

That evening, after the official ceremony was over and the visitors had departed, a small but special celebration party was about to commence in the newly-renovated Lodge at the entrance to the Park. Mrs Bannister and Mr Hicks had been busy preparing for the arrival of the guests, and the Colonel and Miss Ferriday decided that it was time to begin.

"Ladies and gentlemen, children, friends!" The Colonel's voice rose above the hum of conversation. "My sister and I are delighted to welcome you to Tangleton Lodge. In particular –"

"Just a moment, Claude – is everyone here?" Miss Ferriday interrupted in a loud whisper.

"Mr Pegler and Joe are missing, I think," Mrs Davis said, looking up from her task of helping young George Pegler to cope with a full glass of orange squash.

"– and Max, too," added Jenny, who was sitting in a corner seat by the window, sharing a plateful of chocolate biscuits with Kit Pegler.

Mr Davis moved to the door. "I'll see if they're coming." Seconds later, he was back. "Just kicking off their wellies outside," he said. "They've been down at the lake, apparently. Didn't realise what time it was."

"That's Max all over," commented Jenny, reaching for another biscuit.

As though on cue, her brother's beaming face appeared

round the door, binoculars slung round his neck. "The great crested grebes have started mating!" he announced triumphantly.

"An' a pair o' blue tits are buildin' in number seven nes' box!" added Joe, blinking as he entered the lighted room.

"Make room for Mr Pegler, children," Mrs Davis said as the familiar figure appeared in the doorway.

"Ah, there you are, Harry!" the Colonel exclaimed warmly, offering Mr Pegler a glass. "We can't very well start without the warden!"

"Thank ya, sir," Mr Pegler grinned, squeezing into the corner seat between Kit and Jenny. "Move up, you two lasses, an' mek room for a little 'un!"

Colonel Ferriday cleared his throat. "Friends!" he began once more, looking round at the little gathering with a warm smile. "My dear sister has warned me against making a speech, so I will be very brief. This has been a most memorable day. Tangleton Park is now a nature reserve. You – each and every one of you – have played an important part in making this possible. And it will be up to you young people . . ." he turned to Max, Jenny and Joe ". . . to carry on the good work when we old stagers can no longer . . ."

"Thank you, Claude, that will do!" Miss Ferriday piped up, raising her glass. "And now I give you a toast, everyone. Tangleton Park Nature Reserve

"Tangleton Park Nature Reserve!" came the response.

Glasses were raised, the toast drunk, and a happy babble of voices drifted out on the still, evening air, to mingle with a blackbird's richly-warbled nocturne, echoing from the darkening woods.